HOLLYWOOD NYMPH

by

I0680702

CHARLES NUETZEL

WRITING AS "STU RIVERS"

The Borgo Press
An Imprint of Wildside Press

MMVII

CONTENTS

INTRODUCTION

Okay, another tale of the Hollywood type, but with a bit of a different spin and approach. Sure, it relates how a woman climbs from the bottom rung of the success ladder and moves her way up to the top to get the gold ring. That's how stories are generally organized. A character with a strong enough desire to overcome all the hardships and roadblocks that slam down into place to defeat them! One can never tell, for certain, if the author is leading the reader down the road towards a downbeat ending or to a wonderful illustration of success! The not knowing is what keeps everybody struggling through the jungle of words to the last ones.

In this book I offer up a woman who comes to Hollywood and discovers a way to beat a system that devours talent like a hungry tiger. It is overloaded with too many actors seeking the limited roles being offered. It takes more than just talent, or being at the right place at the right time. It is necessary to have the right connections to succeed in such a tough, competitive business. And sometimes it is necessary to do desperate things to create those connections.

Take Ruth:

She was the plaything of any man willing to promote her! But that was the price for Hollywood Stardom!

There are certain elements which make stars. A little guts, a little luck. But more than that, the willingness to do anything to get on top.

Ruth got there—at a price!

She was destined to conquer Hollywood, the hard way, up through the beds of important men. Hers is the story of a brutal woman who used her body; and who used men like most people drove cars—when one wore out, she picked another.

A frank, honest exposé which strips the silver from the silver screen, revealing the tarnished, perverted by-paths that demand full attention on the road to stardom.

That's the promo-copy, but in reality I was interested in studying some ideas based on a rumor I'd heard.

There is a very famous star of old, now long dead, who apparently made stag films long before her name was big enough to appear over the title of a film. Once on top it was not only desirable, but desperately important to her, to get those films out of circulation and destroy the negatives.

At least, that's the story I was told as a young lad by my father, who had heard it whispered somewhat loudly. It was a rumor circulating in the film industry.

True or not, I wondered: what kind of woman might actually get sucked into this kind of ugly trap, and how would she move from that nasty beginning into stardom?

So, I wrote the following book.

—CHARLES NUETZEL
Thousand Oaks, California
August 2006

FOREWORD

This is the story of how one woman made the giant step to fame in the movie industry. It is the story of what makes a star; what a woman must pay—and the kind of woman it takes to be willing to pay that price.

Ruth Browne came to Hollywood in the middle Fifties, and became a well known movie personality. She had those elements necessary to make it to stardom. Call them guts, call them an awareness of being something more than average, or call it merely luck.

Ruth had all of that and more.

She was a woman destined to conquer Hollywood the hard way, up through the beds of important men. Her story is a subtle lesson to young girls who might wish to become Stars. Her climb isn't a pretty story, but it's a frankly honest one, holding back nothing, revealing the perverted byways to stardom.

Not all actors take this route, not all find it necessary, but there are enough who have discovered this difficult climb to be necessary, selectively or not. Some of the biggest named stars have used the casting couch method to some degree or another. The smart ones pick their lovers and connections with selective care and climb up the ladder quite rapidly. Some end up on the streets, sticking needles in their arms and offering tricks to any john who might give them enough money to pay for the next fix. The town can be wonderful to a few, and a trap for others. A few, like Ruth, manage their way through the tangled jungle of egomaniac men and women, who are also desperate to make it to the top at all cost.

Only names have been changed to protect those who might otherwise be hurt by the publication of this book. It is a credit to Ruth that she has been willing to allow the author to record her story, and because of this, even though it was not necessary, we felt it only fair to give her a fictional name. Those, in Hollywood, who know her will remain silent—those who know a little about "Ruth Browne" will possibly guess her true identity; but that does not matter.

The only thing that matters is the lesson to be learned from her experiences.

There are other ways to becoming a Star. There are as many as there are big named actors and actresses. But Ruth has in common with many, the experience of being forced into intimate situations with important personalities.

Nobody would say that what Ruth did was right. But it must be pointed out that her early days as a prostitute was not of her choice. No woman in her right mind would pick such a profession. It was because of her desire to do something more than sell her body to all takers, that moved her toward Hollywood, the one city where her experience might be put to good use.

All women want love. All women want to be admired. Ruth was no different in this way. She came up the hard way; but the end result was success. She sought a better life. She fought for something other than what life had to offer.

We wish to give thanks to "Carlton Turner" for his help in giving us an insight into this complex woman, and for leading us to those people who were intimately involved in her story.

While some events have been written with a freedom of artistic expression, they are based on the most dramatic portions of her climb in Hollywood to her first big chance at Stardom.

As she told me, during one of our many sessions, "Nobody gets to the top in this business without stepping on people—and sleeping with a few. I'm not proud of how I got here—but now that I am, I can only say, thank God it's over!"

And now to her story.

PART I

CHAPTER ONE

The woman appeared tall and well built even in the ill-fitting green dress, as she walked down Main Street away from the bus station. There was little about her which might indicate the international screen personality she would be in a few years. Her hair was a little too long to be in fashion, and a little too mousy to be called glamorous. Yet there was a subtle carriage about her, as she walked down Main Street that revealed an understanding of life most women at twenty lacked.

Her name was Ruth Browne, but in a few years the public would know her under another name. At the moment, all dreams of stardom and fame were distant and unimportant.

She carried a little over-night handbag that held all her worldly possessions. The trip from Kansas City to Los Angeles had stripped her savings down to a few dollars; not enough for a room and meal.

Her full attention was centered on finding a place where she could make some quick money—immediately.

The street was dirty and had the look of dopers, whores, and bums. There were several strip joints, cheap magazine stores, and bars.

After having walked three blocks, she spotted a

small bar that looked suited for her purpose. Without breaking pace, Ruth turned and stepped into the saloon. She sat at the bar and placed her handbag on the floor. Her eyes slowly examined the room, making a careful sweep of the male customers. She smiled knowingly when she spotted a couple of likely prospects. One was a young, nervous man; probably in the service. The other was more mature and looked like a business executive. Either one, she decided, might be an easy mark.

Without apparent effort, Ruth shifted her position on the barstool so that her body was presented in a more sensual inviting way. Her skirt slipped higher, revealing the upper curve of well shaped calves. With a slight action of her long, tapered fingers, she unlatched the top button of her dress. A soft, supple hint of flesh revealed itself. The expression on her face became more brazen.

"Highball," she said in a low, throaty voice, just loud enough to carry throughout the room, without sounding projected. Her eyes made a hurried sweep of her two "marks."

The young man looked up, his eyes met hers and shifted nervously away.

Ruth automatically rejected him.

The older man's gaze leveled with hers—held.

Ruth smiled enough to suggest interest. A flicker of response showed on his handsome face. She looked slowly away, and waited.

"Could I buy you a drink?" a voice asked at Ruth's side.

She turned, startled.

A seedy-looking man was standing there. His thin lips were curled upwards in an eager grin.

16

"No. Sorry," she told him in a soft voice.

"Come on, lady—I seen you lookin' around," he insisted, sitting down beside her.

"Get lost, Buster!" she snapped, nastily.

The man's eyes narrowed. His gnarled hand clamped around her arm. "Look, you little tramp—don't tell me where to get off! What makes you so high and mighty?"

"Let go!" she reached for her handbag and was about to swing it into his face when another man stepped between them.

"Get lost, Buster—like the lady said! " It was the guy she'd been flirting with a moment before.

The two men glared at each other and then the seedy one released Ruth, and moved away.

"Thanks," Ruth said, as her "mark" settled down beside her.

"Think nothing of it." He offered her a cigarette and their eyes met searchingly as he lighted it.

"Name's John Davis, and you're..."

"Ruth." She blew smoke between them.

"New in town?"

"Just arrived."

"Thought so. The handbag," Davis explained. "Where are you heading?"

"Nowhere in particular. Don't know the town." She smiled warmly.

"In for a drink, or something, before settling?" His eyes indicated he guessed her real purpose in being in the bar.

"Or something," she offered, letting it lay suggestively there.

The man grinned. "I could suggest a place." Ruth felt a tingle of satisfaction at that; she'd been right on mark. It was working out faster than she'd hoped it would. "Making an offer?"

"What do you think?"

"That's what I thought," Ruth commented dryly, finishing her drink.

"You don't play around, do you?"

"Is there any reason?" she countered. "You don't play games, either."

"Guess not." He sounded pleased. "Have any objections to...leaving?"

Ruth shrugged: "Why should I?"

It was a record pickup for Ruth. In the past, in Kansas City, it had taken much longer. *But,* she realized, *luck had been with her.*

John Davis paid for Ruth's drink and then took her handbag. They walked out of the saloon and he directed the way down the street. "My place isn't too far from here. How about it?"

"I thought that's where we were heading," she said matter-of-factly.

* * * * * * *

John Davis lived in a one bedroom apartment just east of Hollywood, on Normandie, near Melrose. The apartment was furnished with bright, modern pieces. A long sofa faced one wall and there was a large, red chair opposite a stereo hi-fi set. A small home bar partitioned off the dining room.

She made the normal pleasant comments about the place and looked around for the bedroom.

"Like a drink?" John stepped around the bar, taking a bottle from a shelf.

"Nice of you," Ruth said, sitting on one of the

two barstools. "You didn't have to go to such extremes. Just a couple of bills and..."

He shook his head. "No—none of that, now. After all, you look like a girl who could use a homey atmosphere. And why not?"

"Figure you have a good cheap lay?" she demanded coldly, staring at him.

"No use kidding ourselves," he said, "you wanted to be picked up."

"So—you're quick to observe!"

"And you're new in town. Probably not much money, or you wouldn't be looking for a fast buck." He handed her a highball. "So I figured—"

"You can get me cheap?" she finished for him.

"I'm offering house and home, food and drink. You stay for the night and have breakfast...you have nothing to lose. What more do you want?"

Ruth considered.

He's a real bastard! she thought, *but an honest one. And clever!*

It was too late to back out or to pick up some other mark. He had her trapped and knew it. A nice, velvet lined trap, but still snapped tight.

Then she shrugged. "I guess I don't have anything to complain about. This is as good as I could have gotten on such short order."

"I bet it is," he observed sarcastically.

Ruth bristled. "You're getting what you want— so I get a bed to sleep in. But don't think you're getting anything for free!"

That didn't seem to phase him at all. He simply continued to gaze evenly at her.

They were silent for a short time. Ruth sipped her highball, feeling the warming contents explode

19

in her stomach. It was a strong drink.

Finally she turned to the man and asked: "What were you doing in a dump like that?"

"What you think?"

"Passing the time of night?" she offered dryly.

"No—looking for a woman—like you."

"I knew *that*." She was thoughtful for a moment, then asked: "Why in a crummy place?"

"Why not? Going to some high class place isn't any better and a lot more complicated. Go to a Main Street dive and a guy has a better chance to get what he's after." Then he added: "There were other reasons, too. But I don't want to talk about that."

They were silent for a long while, and Ruth found her thoughts puzzling over John Davis. She looked at him, studying his features more carefully.

He was cleanly cut; his face chiseled and strong looking. There was an intelligent look in his eyes. His body looked hard.

"How long you planning on making the scene? Isn't there a bedroom?"

His eyes whipped to hers, questioningly.

"I've been traveling. I'm a little tired for party build-ups. Either you want something, or you don't. If you do—you'd better make your point pretty soon, or you'll end up with a dull, lifeless girl."

"You certainly don't pull punches," John observed, standing and reaching for her hand.

"It doesn't pay. Marks will play out a girl's last strength...if she'll let him. Not worth it to give out more than a guy pays for. I've had it. I'm near exhausted. And the drink...it's pretty strong. You're looking for a party—I say, let's start, while you'll get your money's worth!"

20

She followed the man across the living room and into the small hallway and through the bedroom door. There was a large double bed in the middle of the room, a dresser to one side, and a chair, in the far corner, piled with clothes.

Ruth looked at the bed and suddenly felt the tiredness move through every nerve and cell. It had been a couple of days since she'd slept in a bed, and this one looked extremely inviting.

Sighing tiredly, she slowly reached around to the back of her dress and carefully unzipped it. The dress fell in a puddle, at her feet. Kicking it aside, she unclasped and slipped out of her bra. Her full breasts burst free, standing firmly self-supported.

Ruth turned and looked at the man. His eyes examined her figure and the expression that welled there was pure animal lust.

She almost laughed as the man reached for her, hungrily covering her lips with his. For a long time their tongues danced together. They slipped slowly onto the bed. Normally she never let a mark kiss her lips, but he had come so quickly at her and she was distracted and drained.

"You're lovely," he murmured, burying his lips into the fullness of her breasts, worrying a tightening nipple.

Ruth felt the stabbing pleasure shooting through her. An excitement bathed her body as the man moved from one nipple to the other. Normally a mark created little sensation in her; it was business, nothing more. But this man was somehow different. And with the right guy she found sex very enjoyable. Once turned on it was total ecstasy.

He's good, she thought, delighted. *He's going to*

be real good!

She felt his hands running along her stomach and then across her thighs.

A shudder of pleasure trembled through her as the man started caressing aside her panties. Then there was a moment, seemingly an eternity, while he stood and undressed. Her eyes watched him, looked over the hardness of his muscles. A burning need ran through her. A gasp sucked down her throat and she reached for the man, now hungrily drawing him to her.

The game of mark vs. prostitute had melted and it was, now, a matter of two animals devouring one another.

His hips drove downwards and she felt the pleasure of him become one with her. Every nerve in her body fired. She writhed, strained, moaned under the driving force of his body. Intense pleasure ripped through Ruth, making her wild with insane joy and ecstasy.

Afterwards she fell back, exhausted.

For a long time she lay there, thinking about herself, and about the man next to her.

It was strange the way things were working out for her, Ruth mused. All her life she'd wanted to come to Hollywood and get a start in the movie industry. With her background and experience, she had been sure it would be only a matter of time before she slept her way to the top. She didn't fool herself about the dangers of falling into a party-girl trap. But a girl gets to know how to handle men after several years of banging it in bed.

It started a long time ago, didn't it? With Big Joe, the foreman who worked for her father. Joe had walked into the barn one day when she was lying half asleep. For weeks he'd been eyeing her. It had been flattering, because he was a large, husky man. That afternoon she had been startled to discover him standing over her, looking down at the exposure of her creamy, youthful thigh.

"You're beautiful, Ruthie," he had told her in a husky rasp. Then his hand had reached down to her thigh, caressing it. The touch was pleasant, and she'd made the mistake of not stopping him.

When his fingers moved upwards, suddenly, without warning, the pleasure had stunned her.

Before she'd realized what was happening, the man was pawing her; then his lips crushed to hers, his body pinning her to the floor. She started to struggle, kicking, trying to scream, but suddenly he seemed to have gone mad with passion.

Ruth could still remember the frantic thoughts that had gone through her mind that afternoon.

Oh, that's good...it feels good...I know what he's doing...and should stop him!

Then she'd gone crazy, clawing at the man, hungrily helping him, until pain broke at her and a gasp escaped from her agonized lips. But with the pain came a sensation she had never dreamed possible.

That was how it had happened that first time. She'd kept quiet about what Big Joe had done, and they had met several times after that. But she quickly became bored with him and sought out other boys and men. The spark, fire, joy of sex had been discovered and she learned how to use that to get things she wanted.

Ruth felt a hand reaching for her stomach, and

lips seek out her soft lips. She turned toward John Davis, drawing him hungrily to her.

CHAPTER TWO

John Davis sat opposite Ruth, at the dining room table. His eyes kept sweeping her body. They hadn't spoken for several minutes, and he didn't say anything until he finished his food.

"Ruth...you need money—am I right about that?" he inquired, reaching for his cup of coffee.

"Everybody needs money. Right now I have to find some means of supporting myself—I do need money, yes," she admitted, pouring cream into her coffee.

"Care how you make it?" he inquired.

"What you think?"

"I could set you up on a good deal. A hundred or so...for just a few hours work."

"I don't think you're a pimp," she announced, looking directly into his eyes. "So what could bring a girl a hundred or more for a few hours work?"

"Movies."

Ruth tensed, nervously. "What you offering? Don't tell me I was picked up by some producer or..."

John laughed and took a sip of his coffee. "Nothing like that...what I have in mind is a certain kind of private movie." The gleam in his eyes flared brighter. He looked at her body, which was naked under the large red robe he'd loaned her.

An icy film of sweat broke over Ruth's body.

"What kind of *private* movie?" She had already guessed, but wanted to have it out on the table, cold and hard.

"Doing the same kind of thing we did last night."

"Stag films, then?" she asked, blandly. Ice hardened at the pit of her stomach. It was one thing to guess what he was suggesting; quite another to deal with it, in reality. At the same time she felt a thrill of excitement wave through her. She had come to Hollywood to get into the pictures and maybe this was one of the best ways to begin. On a practical level it would be a start in the right direction, and better than picking up marks at some bar. It wasn't quite as crude as prostitution. The faking would be for the camera, not some stupid mark. And it paid a lot more.

"It pays good. It'd get you started—give you contacts. With your body...well, you know what I mean. You're a real professional. I was looking for somebody like you last night. When you stepped into the bar, and went through your routine—well, a man in my profession gets to judge people pretty good. I judged you for a pro." He shrugged and then said: "I make it a business to know people—especially woman."

"I didn't think you were a contact man," Ruth admitted.

"I'm not—really. I do a little of this and that. One deal I've got a finger in is this movie. You happened along at the right time." He hesitated and then asked: "Well?"

"What difference does it make? Laying a man in a hotel room for a few bucks or doing it for a camera for a large bill."

"That's the girl! If you work out on this deal— maybe I could line you up on some other things. Ever try dancing for a stag party?"

Ruth shook her head. "Out of my line."

"Doesn't matter. I can fix you up on other deals." He grinned. "After breakfast I'll call Mr. Anson. I think he'll like you."

* * * * * * *

Mr. Allen Anson was a large, fat man with beady eyes and an oily grin. He had been looking at Ruth for a long time as if she were some delightful feast that he'd like to dive into.

"You really pick them, Johnny-boy," he said, without looking at the other man. "She knows the deal?"

John's eyes met Ruth's and then he nodded. "Yes."

"Take off your clothes," Anson ordered in a business like voice.

Ruth felt a shudder. A nagging grind at the pit of her stomach caused a cold sweat to cover her body. Getting undressed in front of a man like this could lead to blatant sex. Not that he was any different from any other crappy mark; only there was something about him that was creepy. She didn't look forward to putting out to Anson; but if that was part of the deal there wasn't anything she could do about it.

Ruth quickly removed her dress and bra. The

man eagerly stared at her body.

"Yes—she'll do fine. Where'd you pick her up?"

"On Main Street. She was hustling. Walked in brazen as Hell. Scanned the bar and sat down. I was pretty sure she'd be a mark for our film. In any case I had nothing to lose, and plenty to gain, by picking her up." John grinned, then lighted a cigarette and slowly turned to Ruth. "Honey, you'll be great."

She turned her attention to the fat man. "You think I'll do?" she inquired, throatily, thrusting her breasts forward.

The man's eyes seemed to grow larger and he stepped forward, reaching out to caress and fondle one breast. "You got them. And they're lovely and real. You let a man lay you in front of a camera?"

A sudden voluptuous tingle slashed at Ruth, and she wasn't sure if it was caused by the man's exploring hand or by the sudden mental image of having sex in front of other people. For a moment she puzzled over the thought, wondering what there could be about it that could excite her.

Her eyes turned to the man and a bitter dislike settled in her mind. He was a pig. Ruth shook her head, and the action bobbed her breast in the man's hand.

She said: "You hand over the money and I'll lay a man in the middle of Hollywood and Vine, at noontime, if there's enough in it for me."

Anson laughed. "I bet you would!" He turned to Davis. "Get lost, Johnny!"

There was a moment of stone silence, nobody moving, and then John Davis left the small office.

Anson turned back to Ruth. His hand hadn't left

her breast. It was clammy with sweat now. "You got some real meat on you, baby. Real meat. If you want this job...you gotta please the right men." He moved closer. "I like you. I could be a lot of help for you. New in town—you need contacts." His hand moved down to her stomach and then edged lower, crudely exploring. "You play ball with me— and I'll do a lot for you. Davis is a nothing."

"You want to lay me—you better talk business, first."

"You want to talk business?" Anson inquired. "A hundred for a film."

"Get lost!"

"What you want? Just in town. Bickering? You get men for a hundred every night?"

"That's different."

"I can do you a lot of good." The man considered, tapping the point of his nose with a beefy finger. "You do a good job—the whole works—and I'll make it three hundred...but, I think you'd better show me what you can do, first."

The man stepped forward, taking her in his arms. She merely blotted out her mind and thought of something else as he assaulted her body.

* * * * * * *

Ruth was sitting in a bar. It was late and she had been sitting there for a long time. John was out taking care of some important business, and for that she was glad. It gave her a few hours to be by herself.

It had been months since she'd felt so dirty and cheap. Every once in a while such guilt plagued her.

She would think about when she'd been an innocent girl, when she had dreamed about love and romance and mentally pictured the knight who would come into her life. She had believed in the romantic fairy-tale myth of love and living happily ever after. How brutally it had been snapped away from her by the discovery that her body needed sex; feasted on it like a starved demon.

You're a tramp, Ruth, so why let it bother you? You've been a tramp for as long as you've been a real woman! You can't escape that.

She took another swallow of the drink in front of her and looked down the bar. There was a young man staring at her. He smiled as their eyes met.

Ruth considered and then shook her head. Not tonight. The afternoon session with Anson had been enough for one day. Tonight she wouldn't bang it for the highest paying mark. In any case, tomorrow she'd be doing it in front of the camera with some fellow "actor".

She wondered what kind of man made stag films; for kicks? Dope? A struggling actor trying to survive? A street kid? A male prostitute?

Well, she'd find out.

For a long time she sat there, downing one drink after another, trying to harden her thoughts about the new, unsettling events that had taken place since she'd arrived in Los Angeles. All so fast. She had lucked out, really. That must was a surprise. She'd planned on picking up men during the first few weeks. It was a nasty bit taking marks from a bar. But in a short time she figured to do it with more class, until she had discovered a connection with the Hollywood people. They had to be around. She'd played the call girl routine several times before, and it paid well. It had seemed the only possible way for her to get fully established in the big city. But the unexpected turn of meeting John Davis was still a little unnerving.

And there was the stag-movie she'd have to play out. No matter how much she'd been arguing with herself, a feeling had been settling deep down in her consciousness that it was a dirty business.

Suddenly she realized the drinks were getting through to her. She didn't want to get drunk. After paying the bartender, she left the bar. For a moment she stood on the sidewalk, listening to the night sounds of the city. She didn't know what to do with herself.

Maybe you're just nervous about tomorrow, she told herself.

After a moment she started down the street, looking into the dark shop windows.

At the next corner she noticed a small theater and turned, moving to it.

Thoughts plagued her as she remembered the job she had to do the next day. The urge, which she'd been fighting all afternoon, to get drunk, suddenly overpowered her. There was only a little over ten dollars left of the money John Davis had loaned her. Not enough to really put on a drunk. Then she remembered the well supplied boozing-bar at John's apartment.

A little less than half an hour later she was in Davis' apartment, helping herself to his supply of rum. Stepping across the room, she flipped on the hi-fl stereo set, looked through a few of the records and picked out one named, *"The Soft Sell,"* that featured Don Bagley on bass.

She settled back and listened to the mellow sounds of the three piece jazz group. The glass was empty by the time the first side had played itself out. She stood, turned the record over and then poured herself another drink.

It was a long time before the booze started to do its work; a long time before she stopped worrying about the next day; a long time before she wasn't bothered by doubts and fears; before she stopped being afraid. By that time she was completely smashed.

* * * * * * *

"Okay, now, Ruthie," Anson instructed, pointing to the cheap sofa. "I want you to lie there, and when the man steps up to you, look excited. Smile, and then say something like: 'Oh, darling, I've waited. I needed you. Something hot, you know.' Then you'll reach for him, and do what comes naturally?" He studied her and then asked: "Understand?"

Ruth nodded, then looked at the camera several feet away. A hard lump was constricted in her throat and a thin veil of sweat covered her body.

It seemed different, now, as she lay on the couch, arranging her nude body in such a way that the camera had a full view of all her feminine charms.

"That's dreamy, honey!"

Yesterday it had been merely an interesting idea she could think about, without really considering how it might be. The three hundred would set her up for a couple of weeks. An easy setup for a day's work. Now she felt an inner uneasiness

Maybe, someday, she'd hate herself for this film, she thought nervously.

Ruth looked at Anson. "How about another drink?" The fat man nodded. "Joe—give the woman a drink."

A young man stepped up with a bottle of whiskey. His eyes stripped down her body with a mixture of interest and embarrassment. She wondered, vaguely, as she took a few swallows of the liquor, what he might be like in bed. He looked young and strong, full of innocent eagerness.

What would her mother think about her being in this kind of picture. Ruth wondered, annoyed at the thought. *Mom was a bitch in heat, too—so what? She was laying everybody on the farm! So, you're like your dear sweet slutting mother!*

"Okay, honey—we're rolling. So look bored. Look around the room, and now run your hands over your body—your breasts, hips, look like you need it—that's right—now, touch your breasts. Remember, you feel hot, you want a man. Look at the camera—directly at it—look hungry—sexually— that's right baby. Act as if the camera is a man, so that every man looking at the film will think you're...right. Oh, Baby, that's wonderful! *You're doing great!*"

Ruth went through the motions, feeling nothing. She couldn't help wondering what it was going to be like with the slob that would lay her in front of the camera.

"Okay, Mack—come on in!"

A tall, seedy looking man stepped toward the

sofa. His eyes moved over Ruth's body.

"Oh, honey," she breathed, "I've been waiting for you—I need it, real bad." She ran her hands over her body and closed her eyes.

The sound of the man undressing seemed to last an eternity. In that few moments she found a wild torrent of guilt attacking her mind.

What was she doing...in a cheap set-up like this? What crummy...how low could a girl get? It was one thing to pick up slobs for a private party—it was something else to do it in front of a camera.

All at once she realized it wouldn't be possible to go through with it. She'd done dirty things before, but this was completely different.

She felt the man move to her, his clammy hands covering her breasts. Panic set in.

Inwardly she fought with herself. Battled a silent war. Then suddenly a choking scream broke from her lips; she twisted away from the man. Jerking from the sofa, she leaped to her feet

The others were too stunned to stop her. Ruth rushed from the room, sweeping up a coat that was draped over a chair. Wrapping it around her, she rushed down the dimly lighted hallway of the cheap hotel in which they were making the film. Voices called after her, but she ignored them.

Ruth kept running until she was outside the building. The city sounds of East Los Angeles crowded around her. She felt a sense of momentary relief.

John Davis rushed to her side, twisting her around.

"What the hell!" he cursed.

Ruth looked coldly into his eyes. "Let go, John,"

34

she demanded in a threatening voice.

"You get the hell back in there. Right now!"

"No. I'm sorry, John. I just discovered I'm not that much of a cheap slut. Maybe a tramp—a slut, if you want, but a classy one! Only not that bad!" She turned, walking away from him.

"You can't do this to a man like Anson—he can be rough!" Davis called after her, but she wasn't listening.

Ruth was walking for a long time before she spotted a bar. She looked at it for a few moments and then made up her mind. She wasn't much worse off than she'd been a couple of days before. Maybe a little better off; she knew a little about the town; and she had *always* known about men. She needed money; a pickup would give her the necessary start.

She walked into the bar. Scanned it. There were three men sitting at the counter. One was old, on the skid-row list. Another looked like a truck driver. The third was just an average Joe-slob.

Nobody could tell she had nothing on underneath the coat, and that was to her advantage. It would be easy to make her point by giving one of the three men a quick look at a naked thigh.

She picked out the husky man who looked like a truck driver. Sitting next to him, she brushed her thigh against his.

The man turned. Stared.

Her grin was inviting.

"Hello, lady," he greeted, smiling.

"How about buying a girl a drink?" she asked. Her thigh pressed into his, in brazen offer.

"Sure—sure, honey. Care where we drink it?"

"All the same with me," she offered, parting the

bottom of her coat so that he was the only one able to see that she had nothing on underneath.

He grinned. As she closed the coat again, he ordered a bottle from the bartender.

* * * * * * *

"I want her found!" Anson was screaming in a violent rage. "And either she plays out the act—or you see to it that she ends in the hospital!"

John Davis looked at the other man, biting down the hard churning at the pit of his stomach. He had begun to like Ruth, and hated the idea of carrying out the other man's orders.

"She cost money...and nobody can do a thing like that to me and get away with it!" Anson cursed.

"Look—if I could make arrangements—can't we let her go?" Davis offered.

"Hell, Johnny-baby—look around you. We had everything set up. Your chick chickened out. You pay—regardless! I'll take it out of your hide if you don't find her and get her back here. You just see to it that she comes back—or both of you'll be damned sorry—believe me. Damned sorry!" The man circled the room with a wave of his arm. "This cost money. Nobody double-crosses me—and you better realize that, sonny!" His eyes squinted, threateningly. "Get her back! Or...you *know* what happens!"

John Davis slowly turned and walked from the room.

He knew it was going to be necessary to get her back—regardless.

It was a point of principle to Anson; and Anson was a man of great principle. There would be no getting around it.

A shudder rushed over Davis as he stepped out into the street. *Find a young woman in a large city...it might be impossible, unless she returned to his apartment, that didn't seem very likely.*

He'd really gotten himself into a spot this time. A real hot one! And possibly a nasty hospital bill. Men like Anson played nasty.

CHAPTER THREE

It was the first time Ruth had ever allowed her-self to really get drunk with a mark. It was a drastic mistake. Her plan had been to roll the guy for what ever he had. She'd never done that before, but times had never been quite as bad as they now were.

But the disgust, the confusion and bitterness had played on her, and the whiskey had flowed down her throat, slowly creating its band of numbness.

The man was a crude lover, but there had been a lot like him in her life. Anson had been much more clumsy. And in her state of mind she couldn't care less.

It was brutal and over much too fast for even her greedy nerves to respond. Afterwards they drank some more and then he claimed her again. He was far too strong to escape without getting physically hurt.

Sleep clouded over Ruth's mind after that, and when she awoke she was alone and sick from a throbbing hangover. She lay there on the bed for a long time, trying to calm her grated nerves and soothe the ache hammering at her skull.

Then memory of where she was, and the events of the day, wedged into awareness.

You really fixed things for yourself this time,

baby, she thought. *Nothing but a hangover for your efforts.*

A nausea worked its way up through her stomach.

Frantically she raced from the bed, making it to the bathroom just in time. After several convulsive movements over the washbowl, she looked at herself in the mirror.

"You're a pretty sight!" she choked out. Her face was pale and had only traces of makeup left. Still it was an attractive face. Her lips were full, dimpled at the corners. Large eyes, bright even through the sickness, stared back. Her high cheeks were drawn and white, her mousy blonde hair mussed.

"Where now, little girl? No clothes—no money. Where now?" she questioned.

After a moment Ruth walked back to the bed, sat down, and buried her face in her hands.

There wasn't much for her to do. She could try picking up another man, bring him up to the room, charge a twenty and then give him a quickie. Or, she could return to John Davis' apartment.

That last thought had only one conclusion: *she'd be in hot trouble with Anson—and...She didn't want to think about that!*

Shrugging, Ruth stood, searched for the coat she had taken from the hotel room and then spotting it on a chair, got up and went over to it. A little while later she was walking along the hallway, then down the steps. It was a cheap hotel, the kind where prostitutes brought men.

Ruth walked through the lobby and out into the street.

It was dark out and from the street's traffic Ruth guessed it had to be past three. For a moment she considered returning to the hotel room. It had been paid for, in advance, by her pickup. Then she shook her head.

She had to think, and many times in the past she had done her best thinking while walking city streets, in the middle of the night. There was a peacefulness about the night world that made it possible to think more clearly.

How long she walked, how many times the problems went through her mind, she didn't know. But after what must have been hours, Ruth was forced to the one and only course open to her. She would have to return to John Davis—and make the film.

* * * * * * *

Ruth had waited for about ten minutes in front of the apartment door before ringing the bell, and then there was a longer stretch of torture until the door opened.

What would John do? Would he be glad to see her? Or want to push her face in?

The door opened and John Davis stared sleepily out. He blinked several times. His mouth dropped. Finally, after several moments, he reached for Ruth, dragging her into the room, slamming the door behind her.

"Where the hell've you been?" he demanded.

"A long story," she announced, tiredly.

"I've looked everywhere! Anson was furious." His face hardened. "You can't walk out on the deal like that. He's ordered you up for a hospital visit."

Terror webbed her insides. "Please—can't you help me?"

John considered: "I could give you the money for a ticket out of town—but Anson would have me sent to the hospital, and you'd never be able to return to L.A...."

Ruth shook her head. "I have to make the film, don't I?"

"Yes. That's the only way." He lowered his eyes. "I'm sorry I got you into this...I didn't think you'd...well, not like the deal."

"I'm sorry." Ruth sat down on the sofa. "Have a drink?"

John went to the bar and returned with two glasses of whiskey. They sat there in silence for a long time and then he reached over and patted Ruth on the shoulder.

"I should hate your guts," he said. "But...you're not the kind of woman a man can easily hate."

"Thanks."

"You're really just a lost little kid."

"Don't fool yourself!" Ruth snapped, angrily. But inwardly she thought: *a real confused and scared kid. You never knew it would turn out like this. You were going to take over the Big City! Ha! That's a laugh! It took you over. And very fast!*

Then her shoulders squared, she sat up straight. *This is only the first round, Los Angeles!*, she told herself. *I've just begun to fight. So you guttered me, this time. Next time—maybe things will be different.*

"John," she said, turning, looking directly at the man. "You have contacts—other than Anson?"

"What can you do—besides the sex routine?"

41

He studied her, carefully.

"I want in the pictures. The *real* thing. I came to Hollywood to get into show business!" she announced evenly.

John blinked, surprised. His face seemed on the verge of laughter, and then, after a moment, he said: "Well...now, if I haven't heard everything!"

"What's wrong with wanting—"

"You don't think you can just step out and become a...oh, *come on!* You couldn't have knocked around like you must have, and believe that all you have to do is walk into Hollywood and take over."

"No. I didn't think it'd be simple. But that's what I plan on doing!"

"It takes years. Years of hard work, and the right contacts. A bit of acting and experience; and.... It takes more than just sleeping your way up, which you seem to think is the only thing necessary. Well...*for God's sake!* You *must* be kidding!" John exploded, staring down at her.

"I'm serious!" Ruth bit her lower lip. "You must know *somebody* that could help me."

"You *are* serious."

"Yes. I mean to make it. No matter what it costs. No matter what I have to do. If I have to keep out of the hospital by doing that bitching film for Anson— I'll do *anything* to shove it down his dirty little throat! I'm going places in Hollywood. If you want to point me in the right direction—I won't forget you!"

A mild smile moved the corners of the man's lips. "Okay—maybe I could set you in the first direction. You're great looking...and talent and all that is second to timing and contacts...I *do* have contacts. But that's all. I can't pull any strings. I can't even get you a contract—or anywhere in the film industry. But I do know a few Hollywood boys who might take a liking to you..." He was thoughtful and then nodded to himself. "Yes, maybe I'll make you pay off...maybe I'll make you pay off, after all."

"What's that mean?" she demanded bitterly, standing, glaring at the man.

He turned so fast on her that Ruth was startled, almost frightened.

"You cost me a commission with Anson. He cut me off—completely. Said it was all my fault. And you won't be making a dime out of the deal now. You might as well get your mind set on that. Yesterday's little walk-out cost...not what he was going to pay you—but nobody walks out on Anson, and he's determined to make you pay. So...the deal is for payment on his pride. Either a hospital stay—or the film. But I could make a little for both of us—if you want to play it my way."

"What does that mean?"

"I can introduce you to some contacts—but for money you'll sleep with them."

"So what's so shocking about that? I can make my impression on them—my own little way!" And she added to herself: *her own deals with them—and dump John Davis, when the time came.*

* * * * * * *

It was an agony of shame and nausea for Ruth Browne. They went through the scene like it had been outlined to her, the day before. The man came

43

into the room, she said how much she'd been waiting for him, and then he undressed and moved to
her. She went through the actions of ecstasy, and
when the man stepped away from her, Anson said
"Cut".

"Now, baby, you'll do it again—the last parts,
for close-ups!"

The camera and the crude lights were re-set and
what went on after that disgusted her so much that
she had to force her thoughts to think of other
things. Ruth knew that she was in a semi-state of
unconsciousness when it was over. The mental agony had numbed her brain.

Then John Davis was shaking her.

She looked up and almost felt an emotional response toward the man. The expression of compas-
sion on his face revealed his feelings. It startled
Ruth, because she thought of John Davis as a hardened bastard.

Slowly Ruth moved from the couch, ignoring
the men around her.

"Nice job, baby," Anson called.

She passed the fat man without saying a word,
and went into the bedroom, gathered her clothes,
dressed and then returned to the living room. Anson
was in the corner talking to Davis and the cameraman. She stepped up to him and said: "You're a
goddamned bastard!"

Turning, Ruth walked out of the apartment and
down the hall.

John Davis followed her. "That was a foolish
thing to do."

"He deserved it!" she announced, bitterly.

"You're lucky he laughed it off."

44

"He's lucky I didn't cut the cops on him."

"God, honey—don't do that!"

"Don't 'honey' me, John. I'm not in the mood."

They walked down the steps, without saying anything. Once on the street, John Davis asked: "Where you going?"

Ruth looked at him, considered. "I want to go out and get drunk."

"But you don't have any money...is that it?" She shrugged.

"I'll loan you something."

"Why be nice to me?"

"I like you."

"You think you can make a mint out of my body—pimping?" she demanded, coldly. She neither disliked John nor liked him. He was a man— nothing more or less. She considered again. "How about coming with me?"

John blinked, puzzled.

"I want a ball. Want a ball with me?" she asked.

"I'll loan you the money—you don't have to ask me along."

"How nice. Why the consideration?" she asked, acidly.

"I think you've had a hard enough day of it."

"Yes. But it's about time I split for a little fun. Real life fun. Something that I can feel in my guts. Something that will stab through me like electric fire. That's what I want. You're as good as any other lay. Maybe better than some."

The man blinked, again. His face drew tight, serious. "You don't hand out the compliments."

"Why should I?"

"You don't like men, do you?"

"Why should I? They're bastards—all of them! I've seen the worst! Why should I give a damn about them?" She studied him silently and then asked: "Are you coming with me or not?"

"Maybe."

"It'll cost," she warned.

"You don't bend, do you?"

"Not a goddamned inch!"

John laughed, placed an affectionate arm around her, and said: "We're two of a kind."

"Hell we are!" She laughed, almost happily. "Where to?"

"A bar—a hotel room—a bed. Drunksville—and Sexville."

"I shouldn't think that'd be what you'd want. Not after this afternoon." He led the way to his car.

"Why not?"

"Well, most women who play the game the way you do, don't like sex."

"I like it. That's the reason I play it. At least, I like it the normal way. That thing back there—I'd give anything if it would wipe itself out of my memory. It had to be done—if only I'd known that yesterday...but that's over." She slipped into the car and waited until John had gotten behind the driver's seat. "I should hate you for having gotten me into it. But..."

"So, let's forget it?" he suggested.

"Let's. And it won't happen again. Either. A film like that—or me walking out."

* * * * * * *

It was like swimming through a sea of fog. *How*

46

many times before had she been in that fog? Ruth wondered, thrilling to the man's naked caresses.

So many times you've lost count. You're with a man, and his hands are becoming a part of you; they are becoming a caressing heated part of you, as they run along your body, creating the sensations they were meant to create.

Who is it this time?

She couldn't remember, at first. Then, when memory came, the remembrance of what she'd done that afternoon slapped across her mind and she swallowed it into a dark nothingness.

Her thoughts wandered away. Sensation. Clouds. Touches.

Pleasure. Excitement firing every nerve.

A hand slid across her thighs, hesitated. Searched.

Then went away.

His mouth moved over her body, searching. Kissing.

Exploring.

John Davis is a good lover. You'll have to give him that *much!*

No! Don't think about that. You don't want to think about John Davis.

Just think about the hands. The caressing, searching hands. The lips moist and warm. The wine of his kisses covering your body, drowning you in wild pleasure.

She felt a body move to hers.

Every muscle tensed, waiting. Thrilling in the waiting. A movement. Madness! Movement. Rhythm. The hammering weight of a man's form. Powerful. Oh, God. He'll give me a baby!

What made her think of that? Back somewhere in her past. The first time.

Forget.

Oh, God. He's good. I didn't think he'd be that good. He's good. It's going to be fun being a woman.

Forget.

Her mind wandered. Froze suddenly. Ecstasy. Insanity.

Blackness.

The world spun.

Ruth reached for the bottle on the bedstand. Gulped. The whiskey burned down her throat. She swallowed more liquor. Waited.

Where was she? Ruth wondered. The room was cheap. The smell of it attacked her throat. She gulped more whiskey. *Where'd she picked up this slob?*

Ruth turned and looked at the man and saw John Davis and remembered where she was. The man was naked. She looked at his body. He was good. That much she had to say about him. Very good.

Ruth raised the bottle against her lips and gulped it empty. With a sigh, she slumped down on the bed, the bottle slamming to the floor.

The world spun and suddenly she was aware of her hands searching over a man's form. It had no identity.. It was a man who could give her pleasure, and that was all that mattered.

Oh, you like sex, don't you little girl. You really like it. You've liked it since you were a girl—since that first time.

And all those other times.

She moved down against the man. Movement.

Every nerve was baked in molten liquid.

Time blurred. She was walking in the night. The man beside her was supporting her weight. Laughter sounded in her ears.

"You're a ball, Ruthie," John Davis whispered. There was music coming from somewhere, but she couldn't locate it. Then suddenly Ruth realized that time had slipped. Awareness had blackened out. They were in a bar, dancing. She felt the man's body against her.

"When did we leave the hotel?" she asked.

"About an hour ago."

Ruth considered that. She couldn't remember. But now her head was clear. "What happened—to the boozing?" Only with control was she able to keep her words from slurring.

"We came out for some drinks. You were hungry."

"We ate?"

"Don't you remember?" He laughed at the sound of his words.

Ruth laughed. "We're shrunk!"

He squeezed her body tighter against his.

"Let's split?" she murmured.

"A drink, first?"

Ruth nodded.

They went to the bar. Ordered drinks. She had a double Martini. She gulped it down. "Another." Another one came. She worked on it a little more slowly. The world was beginning to close in on her. Dizziness.

"Shyother?"

"Smum more?" John's voice inquired from the spinning world.

Somehow she managed to nod her head. The drink appeared. She finished it off. Staggered from the stool.

Arms helped her from the floor. The darkness was spinning, spinning around and around.

Ruth didn't know how long the black night was closed in on her brain. It seemed forever and at the same time not more than a minute.

Lips were playing hungrily on her.

The bed was a rolling sea under her; a storm that was attempting to drown her. Sensation was distant. Pleasure was numbed. The man's body moved away and she relaxed with a tired sigh Something dim within her mind told Ruth that it was over. The spree had finished itself. It wasn't any more fun. She'd go to sleep, now, and when she awoke the world would be reality again

No! No! Not reality! a voice screamed in desperation

Ruth argued with the voice: *You have to face the struggle someday. Might as well get started again.*

Thoughts drifted, blurred, darkened. She was dropping down, slowly gathering speed, dropping through infinity. Her ears rang; her head throbbed; her body ached.

Ruth was aware of her stomach convulsing, of running, of dropping her head into a dark, stinking well, and then standing, staggering, finding a bed and falling down onto it.

Dizziness whirled her brain. Thoughts began to gather in the semi-darkness. Then light splattered before her eyes.

Ruth sat up in bed.

John Davis was standing by the window, looking out at the morning sun. He turned as a moan broke from her lips.

"Morning, honey."

"Hell—glad you didn't say 'good'!" she exploded, pressing her hands to her throbbing head.

"Hangover?"

"What you think? A splitting one, but I'm afraid I'll live." She managed a smile. "We had a ball, didn't we?" she questioned.

"Don't you know?"

"Hell, of course." She looked at the man and felt a light sense of affection. "You're a pig—but a nice one."

"Thanks," he laughed. "Thanks a lot."

"Think nothing of it. I'm not handing out flowers. Just a thank you. That's all you get from me, anyway." Ruth moved from the bed. "I need a headache powder and I need a little breakfast. Think that can be arranged?"

"Something like that," John told her. "I could use something, myself. Get dressed and we'll face the world."

Yeah, she thought, *face the world, and the hell there is in it.*

Ruth turned and looked at him. "You're a good lay, John. But I hate your guts."

"Thanks, baby. I figured as much. We're a good match, like I said. We'll make a good partnership." His eyes looked greedy.

"Don't count on it!" she snapped, dressing.

"I'm not—but you'll play, for a while. You might go places, at that. There's something about you that catches on with a man—if you use it right...all I ask is a little return. My cut."

"You got your cut—last night, and if you can squeeze anything more out of me in the next days. After that—don't say I didn't warn you!"

"You're a hard bitch, Ruth. A real hard one. And I don't know why I don't just use you—it wouldn't be too difficult—but I have the feeling you'd come out on top, in either case."

"You're damned right. Goddamned right! Try to con me the wrong way—and I'll cut your throat!" The look the man gave Ruth convinced her that he actually believed that warning.

Despite herself, Ruth smiled. "Okay, sorry for the cold cut. You're okay, John. A bit of a slob—but you have a sense of ethics. That's something, at least. Now, let's go out and have something to eat— then, the world! If you want to make a little slick bill or two—you'd better get to work finding somebody to introduce me to." As they walked out of the room, Ruth found it almost impossible to make herself really hate the man. In fact, there was something about him that actually touched some inner nerve; a caring for him as a person. Maybe they were alike, in some way.

What's happening to you, Ruthie? she questioned, silently. *Getting soft?*

PART II

CHAPTER FOUR

It was a small office for a Hollywood producer, but Carlton Turner wasn't a flashy man when it came to business. In his personal life he lived in style; but that was something different. Business was a means to make money to *live*. Yet, strangely, his business of making cheap, successful movies had become more than a matter of turning out hack films. He considered his product in terms of art and science. Maybe the art wasn't "arty," but the science of moviemaking was one of his perfected talents. He was small-time, but successful.

He looked at the two men sitting opposite him, across the worn desk. They were first rate con-artists.

The better looking of the two, John Davis, had a style about him that almost pleased Carlton. Davis was young, but had knocked around. It showed in the man's alert eyes, the way he phrased his words.

"Look, Mr. Turner," he was saying, leaning forward, tapping the photo of the beautiful blonde. "You have the know-how, the means, we have a woman who will fit the part perfectly. Besides that, you could do a lot of big things with her. She has talent. She has good looks. And what's more important, she's willing to sleep with the right people."

Carlton looked at the photo. The woman was Ruth Browne, some unknown broad who was trying to edge her way into show business. Probably the only talent she had was pleasing men in bed.

He considered her body, letting his eyes flow over the seductive lines of her breasts, her voluptuous hips and thighs.

He had already made up his mind about her.

"I don't know, boys," he said, bored sounding. "I could give her the bit—it's merely a walk-on—but..."

"We'll cut you in for a good percentage—if she goes big," Baker, the larger man, said.

"A cut of what? She's nothing. If getting exposure in one of my films starts her out—well...I'll get my cut," Carlton pointed out.

He studied the pudgy man. Baker was in the call-girl business; and anything else he could cut into. A nasty little fellow who considered himself power—but was nothing more than a small time promoter. Carlton didn't like the setup. His eyes drifted once more to the photo. The woman was outstandingly seductive; young and lovely. There was an awareness in her eyes that only belonged to a female of thirty. She would be good in bed. Even if she faked it; she'd be a wonder for any man to enjoy. That element was obvious; and if it came across on film she'd be a nice addition to any movie selling sex, even if only on a classy level. In fact, there was the element of classy sexuality that was appealing. Interesting.

"Look," Davis said. "All we're asking is for you to invite her to the party—give her a look-see—take her to bed, if that's what you want. Hell, if you don't think you could do anything for her, forget it. We've been getting a lot of money off her, in the past six months. Just look her over. That's all we ask."

Carlton smiled. How many times had he been given such offers? The casting couch was easy to mount any number of lush, easy to have, wannabe actors—male or female. So many promoters and agents had been in his office, offering bed-sessions with their clients, that he'd lost count years ago. What amazed him was the fact that he even listened to these two guys. They were crude; completely unprofessional in their approach. Well, crass, at least. Certainly blunt, not subtle. At least it was on the table, no questions left unanswered. Nothing subtly implied like some slicker operators.

The photo attracted his eyes. He'd been somewhat fascinated the moment he saw the woman's image, but skilled enough to hold back any real reaction. If she was anything like that vision then it might well be worth his time to give her some swift consideration in the flesh. A picture could be fixed, faked, shaped; the real thing couldn't hold the illusion for very long.

That was the answer. On the surface Ruth Browne was quite lovely; the most attractive girl he'd seen for a long time. He might even enjoy getting to know her better—intimately. If it came to that.

"Okay," he finally said, "I'll look her over. No promises, though."

* * * * * * *

It was a party like many other parties that Ruth had gone to in the last six months. Important Hollywood producers, important Hollywood stars, unimportant starlets and casting directors and hangers-on. It was one of those affairs where the struggling met the VIPs, hoping to get their big break. Homosexuals made advances to young male "starlets"; lesbian VIPs attempted it with the young women. Some made their points. Ruth ignored them. She was here for a purpose; planned and prepared for in advance. John Davis was busy attracting her mark, a small-time producer who was interested in considering her for a part in his latest cheap production. She had to please the man, in any way he desired. There was a good chance that it would pay off. So John had said. So John had told her before about other such male "small shots"! Though there was something different tonight; a slight edge, something classier. And John's attitude had even reflected a sense of real excitement, as if this were actually "it"!

Tonight could be a big step in her career.

Ruth considered the last months with a feeling of distaste. A lot had happened; a lot of men had slipped in and out of her life. There had been money—but most of it had stuck to John's fingers. That didn't bother Ruth. A time would come when she would be cashing in on her efforts, and the payoff would be big. For six months she had lived with John, giving her body to him when it wasn't being sold out to some other slob. This was all better than picking up street marks. At least there was a better selection—and her "pimp" was somewhat caring about her in a personal way. They were almost friends. And she could dump John any time she wanted. Most of the money she'd made was gathering interest in a small savings account.

Ruth reached toward the punch bowl. She poured herself a cup of champagne. This was her third drink and she was beginning to feel the effects.

She looked around the large, crowded room. None of the other parties had been this impressive. This was an expensive Beverly Hills home; and the kind of place she hoped to someday live in.

She shrugged. *It'll take time, little lady. Just hold on—you're going to get this—and a lot more!*

John Davis stepped up to her with a tall man at his side.

Ruth looked at the handsome stranger as he was introduced to her. His hair was curly black and receding. His features were fine and sensitive. Steel gray-blue eyes studied her.

"This is Carlton Turner," Davis announced. "He's the man I've told you about."

Yes, Carlton Turner, small time producer, playboy and rich, she thought. *A rich sucker for a sharp girl! Obviously smart, well-heeled and a possible step up for her.*

John Davis politely disappeared.

"I've heard a lot about you, Mr. Turner," Ruth offered, letting her lips reveal just a suggestion of a smile. The smile was a trick John had taught her. She had learned a lot in the last six months.

"Call me Carl, sweetheart," the man instructed, placing an arm around her shoulder, leading her across the room, through the party crowd, and into a large private office. "Davis tells me you're interested in getting into pictures." The man closed the door behind him and latched the lock. "I like to have interviews in private," he explained, turning and letting himself take in her full figure. It was an automatic, almost professional examination; without too much seductive intent. The new red dress hugged her body, and boldly revealed her breasts in a classy and seductive manner. She knew men found it difficult to keep their eyes off her neckline. "Where's John been keeping you?"

"Oh, I've been around."

"I bet you have!" the other laughed, implication heavy in his voice. He stepped across the room to a small desk. He sat down and studied Ruth. "How long you been in Hollywood?"

"About six months," she frankly admitted, taking a seat opposite him. For some reason she felt this was a no-bull interview; and played into that mood.

The man studied her for a long time in silence, his eyes repeatedly pausing at her thrusting bust line.

"You're attractive enough," he offered, coldly. "What else do you have to offer besides sex?"

"What else is there to offer, Carl?" She said it in such a way as to imply intimate promises to him.

He shook his head "A lot."

Silence.

Ruth considered what she knew of this man He had money and had created several small-time stars. He was the type of guy who had his finger in a little of everything. He was cold-blooded, careful, and intelligent. Ruth had been taking a course in acting and singing and dancing. She'd been putting out to the instructor to pay for the lessons. The instruction

60

had included polishing her approach to men. Ruth had been amazed about how much she had to learn about dressing, about social manners, and about making intimate passes, without being too obvious. Her hair had been cut short and bleached.

"Don't think, Miss Browne, you can wiggle your hips at me, and have me dancing eagerly around you, and don't think that the public can be sold on just the sex routine. Beautiful, sexy women are...a cheap commodity in this town. It's a complicated job to promote a woman. It takes effort, time and skill. Don't think you can sleep your way up, either. Hot—and cold—sex on the casting couch is routine. It takes more than that to get any further ... a lot more. Too many of you...ladies...are swift lays for a lot of, quite frankly, small execs who used them and dump 'em. If you get my meaning. A man will let you go to bed with him—and then throw you out afterwards. A lot end up being handed around before they end up on the streets, all but giving it away for mere survival or a needle in the arm."

"Why you telling me this?" she inquired. "That's pretty basic, obvious stuff."

"Because you interest me. And because— certain arrangements are in the offing."

Ruth felt surprise edge through her. She hadn't known anything other than what John Davis had told her. She was to play up to this man, make it good, and possibly he would become seriously interested in her.

"That's news to you, isn't it?" Carlton inquired.

Ruth considered; then decided. "Yes. I didn't know about any arrangements." She hesitated, then asked: "What kind of arrangements? And who made them?"

He was silent for a moment, then finally sighed. "It's really not important to tell you."

"But I'd like to know. Don't you think I should know what's going on behind my back?" she countered, pulling out a pack of cigarettes from her small evening purse.

Carlton laughed. "Maybe. Maybe."

Ruth lighted her cigarette and took a deep drag, her eyes frozen to the man's.

"Davis—and Hal Baker...but I don't think you know anything about Baker, either, do you?"

Ruth felt ice tensing her stomach. She was amazed at what he was telling her. "No...no, I don't!" Her voice was thick with irritation; and coldly chilled.

"Baker is in promotion—even if you don't know it—he's got a piece of the operation. And he's offering me a chunk—if I'm interested in you."

Alarm showed on her face. It was impossible to hold back the surprise. And the anger. All she had known was that John Davis had been having her sleep with men, collecting a little on the side for himself, and arranging more meetings. She suddenly felt like a puppet. She couldn't remember having slept with Baker.

"What kind of piece is being cut out of me?" she questioned, coldly.

"Nothing yet." For a long moment he considered her, then suddenly seemed to make a decisions. "For some reason I feel the need to be blunt with you. The deal all depends on how I react. If a deal swings through the way your backers hope it will...you'll be cut up pretty nice. But you'll know then, because contracts will be signed." The man lighted a cigar. "They haven't been keeping you very well informed, have they?"

She merely shrugged, letting her eyes continue to stare directly into his. There was no seductiveness even suggested. The man was all business and she instantly reflected the same hard-line mood.

He asked: "What have they been doing to you?"

"What you mean?"

"Been pimping you around?"

His question surprised Ruth; but she'd been around enough to feel no sense of embarrassment. "What business is it of yours?"

"None—as of yet. It will be my business if I decide to use you."

"How cute. You make a lady feel like a product."

"That's what you'll be. Nothing but a product. Without feelings, without emotions, without individuality and without thoughts. You'll be a puppet on a string, speaking written lines, going through written actions—on and *off* screen. You'll be a damned creation. I'll be only the beginning. If I use you for my next film you'll make a slight noise in Hollywood, and other people will notice. Then you'll be making other contacts who'll take a large slice out of you—and if you happen to make it all the way, all of us will be up there with you. If not— you'll continue making crap films with me. You'll make little money and be signed for seven years. Your life won't be your own. You'll just be another starlet-on-the-string, making crummy pictures."

"Don't kid yourself, Mr. Turner," Ruth snapped,

suddenly angry, once more her old self. "Nobody strings me, for long! I'll slash your soul out!" The emotions in her voice seemed to startle the man.

He stared at her for a long time, his mouth open, eyes wide. "Well, you do have fire, don't you?"

"You Goddamned better believe it!" The fury was seething through Ruth like hot, hateful fire. "I might have been pushed around these last months. And some bastards might think they could play cheese-cake with me—cutting me in pieces, but they have a surprise waiting for them. Nobody cuts me up—unless I want it. And nobody tells me where to get off. I'm free—and I'll stay free. *I'll* write the lines and *I'll* write the scenes. If Davis and this slob Baker think they can rub my face—pull strings and make me dance out pretty money for them—they have a surprise coming."

Carlton had recovered a little and leaned back, a half amused expression on his face.

"I don't push. And I don't beg. If you think you can cut me up in pieces, you can take your crummy offers and shove them up deep!" She spat out the last words like bullets.

"Okay—okay! I'm convinced!" Carlton laughed. "You're a wild one, aren't you?"

"More than *you* can handle!" she announced. All the gloss that the last months had painted on her had ripped off, and she was the old Ruth Browne who had arrived in Los Angeles half a year before. It had taken her several minutes to realize what had actually been happening in the last months. It had been a shock. She'd gotten to the point where she trusted John Davis—and that was a mistake she promised never to make again.

Boy, are you a dumb one, she thought, angry with herself.

"I thought you might react like that. The minute I saw you—well, a man gets to know his women," Carlton announced, standing and walking around the desk. "I know you. Know you like I know the palm of my hand. You're too smart for Davis and Baker. I figured the minute you discovered what was happening you'd blow the cards."

"That's why you told me?" Ruth asked, puzzled, mentally backing down. The man was somewhat different from those she was used to dealing with.

"That's why," he admitted in a warm voice.

"Well, where does that put me? Where now?"

"Where do you want it to put you?" the man inquired.

Carlton didn't look like a fool. But the point was, which way was he playing it? Into Davis' hands—or hers. Or maybe just down the middle.

The shock of discovering she had been used so blatantly was still numbing her mind. Davis had played it close and careful. He'd made the contacts, and the introductions. She'd gone along with him, because there wasn't anything better to do. Both of them had made a little spending money. She owed the man something—in a way. If it turned out that John Davis deserved some kind of payment, he'd get it, later, when she was in a better position to give him *what* he actually deserved.

And you, Mr. Carlton Turner! What kind of damned game are you trying to play with me? she asked herself. Well, look at it his way! He sees this girl who is being pushed around, used. And he says to himself that maybe he could use her like the others had—but a little more skillfully, more subtly. This Carlton was a slick operator.

Come on, girl, you know you want to play ball with him. Just that you want to know what kind of "ball" it is. But what difference does it make? Now that you're alerted, you'll be watchful. He can push you up another step.

"I'll warn you, Carl," she began in a sultry voice, letting her eyes bore deep into his, "you aren't going to be pushing me around. *And you might be sorry!*"

The man laughed. "I don't think so. But I like your nerve. You've got guts. The kind that might make it all the way to the top." He was thoughtful, serious. He stepped up to Ruth, placed an arm around her shoulder. "What say we celebrate?"

"What?" she inquired, sharply.

"Our little private deal."

"And what is that?"

His eyes widened and a new respect welled there. "On an honest level. Dumping Davis and Baker. What else? Let's be frank. Start fresh. You like a drink on that?"

"A drink. But I don't think we're sharing a bed—if that happens to be what you meant!" This latter was a gamble, she knew that, yet felt it might work to her advantage. "That isn't part of the deal— at least at this point!"

Carlton's eyes narrowed. "No man likes that kind of line."

"You aren't supposed to *like* it. To be honest, I don't trust you any more than I trust Davis or this...Baker you've been telling me about! For all I know you've been playing a very clever game.

Maybe Baker doesn't even exist. And for that matter..."

"Okay—okay I don't get you!" He stepped back, away from her. "Some package you are. You're introduced to me—with implied promises. I play it bluntly honest with you, believing you'll like it." The man's voice was angry and his eyes fired as they looked down the full length of her body. "And now you slap my face!"

"And I don't know if you wouldn't just have your fun and call it a day! What's to stop you?" Ruth inquired. A sinking feeling settled through her. Maybe she'd been wrong playing it hardball. She really didn't have anything to lose by going to bed with him. On the other hand, she told herself, she had nothing to lose by *not* going to bed with him.

"Now—what you want? A signed contract? Don't be childishly stupid!" Carlton cried dramatically, waving his hands in the air. "Business is done at parties like this...with spoken agreements. A handshake is the most respected agreement in the world!"

"And the most often broken," Ruth pointed out, seriously.

There was a long, stony silence, and then Carlton's lips began to smile. Just the suggestion of a smile formed at first, then finally he was grinning, his eyes full of amusement. "Oh, boy, girl! You've got a charm about you. A real charm. I don't think many men could cut through you—could they? At least not more than once."

"Damned right!" she exclaimed, looking carefully at him. Carlton was an extremely attractive male animal, with a lot of sexual charm. She considered changing her attitude. Maybe it didn't make any difference either way.

She said: "Want to start over?" Stepping closer to Carlton, Ruth slid her arms around his neck.

"What's this?"

"A girl can change her mind, can't she?" Ruth questioned in a low, throaty voice, bringing her lips close to his.

"You devil!" Carlton laughed, kissing her lips. The kiss was long and probing; their tongues raced at each other, doing battle. The taste of the man sent excitement through Ruth, and the full feel of him straining against her found herself reacting. Her lungs burned and the nerves at the back of her head seemed to go rigid.

Finally the man pulled away, staring down at her. Neither of them said anything for a long time. Then, finally, the man let out a long, exhausted sigh. "You're a real woman! I'll give you that much, Ruth. That much I'll give you, free. Anything else you get from me you'll have to work for."

"Even tonight?" she questioned, femininely.

"Tonight?" The man seemed puzzled.

"Aren't you going to...?"

"Oh, that. Not tonight. I can't leave my guests that long. I think maybe I'll keep you for something special. How about tomorrow evening? Dinner and...the works?"

Ruth grinned, happily.

* * * * * *

That night Carlton surprised himself by not ending up in bed with one of the many willing woman at the party. When the last guest was gone, he stepped up to his small home bar and mixed himself a drink.

His mind turned to the young woman he'd met earlier. Maybe he should have had her stay the night.

No, he thought, *it was better the way he'd arranged it.*

Ruth Browne was a strange, bewitching female. Not many women attracted him the way she had. It wasn't so much her body—though that was reason enough to be interested—but more the vibration around her; a subtle vibrancy which reached out and grabbed at something deep inside him. She had guts; but he'd known other women like that; taken them to bed and forgotten them.

Why was he taken by this Ruth Browne? Was there any logic or reason behind it?

Carlton downed his drink and then walked to his bedroom. As he undressed, his mind kept puzzling over his actions with Ruth.

She had hit him where it hurt the most. Her fire, spitting out as if she didn't give a damn. Quite impressive.

Maybe that intrigued him. The first moment he'd laid eyes on her he'd been hypnotized. Maybe it was his inner ability to recognize star qualities in a woman. He felt certain that she had them.

Carlton shook his head as he slipped under the bedcovers. He didn't like the set-up with Davis and Baker. They were playing games behind Ruth's back. But that could easily be taken care of. He'd offer them a flat fee, and get them out of the picture. That was, if things worked out.

Carlton found it hard to escape his thoughts about Ruth. He lay there for a long time thinking about her, wondering about his quick responsive reaction to her. It didn't make sense. He'd never been in love, and didn't believe in it. Love had always seemed a brain-washing emotion; without logic. Yet, maybe it had been a form of "love" at first sight. Certainly fascination.

He laughed at himself. "Sex at first sight, man!" he said out loud. "So you're saving her for a special evening—to make the most of it. That's the only thing that happened. Stop trying to make something out of nothing."

She was going to be a special evening to remember and enjoy; maybe later an affair.

An intriguing woman.

A little after that he found sleep, convinced he'd discovered the answer to his mental puzzle.

* * * * * * *

Ruth felt nervous and jumpy all day. She actually felt excited about what was going to happen that evening. John tried to give her advice on how to behave with Carlton, but she told him to shut up.

"What's gotten into you?" he demanded, angrily.

"Nothing—nothing!" She had decided to remain silent about what she'd learned of John's side-deals with Mr. Baker, until she'd had a chance to get her nails locked firmly into Carlton Turner. He looked like a first-rate mark to her. Tonight would be a full test of her abilities to control a man, and make him want more. It was only a fine line between a one-

70

night stand, and a prolonged affair. Some how she realize it might be very important to direct him towards a longer relationship.

In the afternoon, Ruth had several Martinis before getting dressed for her date. Then, when seven-thirty arrived, she called a cab. A little later she was stepping into Carlton's large Beverly Hills home. He greeted her with a cocktail and a gentle, intimate kiss on the cheek. The conversation was general and social, having nothing to do with the business that had brought her to his home.

Later, after several more drinks, they went out to dinner in Beverly Hills, at the *Islander,* which served tropic rum drinks and tropic foods. It was late when they returned to his home and went upstairs to a small, private room.

The room was designed for seduction not for sleeping. There was a large bed in the middle of the room, but no dressers were in evidence. A small bar-cabinet was in one corner.

"You aren't very subtle, are you?" she inquired, laughingly, as the man slowly closed the door.

"Should I be?" Carlton turned and stared at her.

Ruth shrugged. "It doesn't matter to me—considering...but surely there must be some women who..."

"Those women are out, in either case!" he coldly announced, stepping across to the small bar-cabinet. "Want a drink?"

"Might as well make the best of things," she commented, moving to the bed and sitting down, testing the softness.

Carlton reached behind the cabinet and a moment later soft music floated through the room.

"Pretty nice," Ruth admitted. "Bed, drinks, and romantic music."

As he was fixing the drinks, Ruth felt her mind being slowly and subtly affected by the setting.

It was one of the few beautiful bedrooms she had ever been in. It was made for a romantic interlude; no holds barred. She had to hand the man that much. He had things pretty nice for himself. Considering his reputation as a playboy, she decided he had earned the title.

"Here's to a nice finish," he saluted, as his eyes moved over her body.

"Tell me something," Ruth said, after having taken a strong swallow of the scotch and water.

Carlton sat down beside Ruth, his leg just touching hers.

"Are you always so sure of women?" She spread her arms wide to take in the whole room.

"The ones I bring up here, yes," he admitted.

"That must be pretty nice—for you, I mean. Being so sure of what you're going to get." The sharpness in her voice surprised Ruth as much as it did the man.

He asked: "You don't like it, do you?"

"What? The room? I think it's beautiful. What else would a woman want—for romance?"

"But it offends you?"

"It shouldn't!"

"Then—it's me?"

"Nothing like that. To be truthful, I don't know why I said that. There's no reason a man shouldn't be thoughtful about romancing his women. Just that I've never entered this level of social mating!"

Carlton's laugh broke through the stilted atmosphere, and Ruth was suddenly laughing too.

"I'm really sorry. Just that I expected something a little more cold—something—maybe not so ready, willing..."

Carlton placed a gentle hand on Ruth's shoulder. "You know something, Ruth."

She turned her eyes up to his and was surprised by the look of sincerity on his face.

"What?" she inquired.

"I *was* going to take the offering on the altar of promotion, dump you and your boys—and let it go at that..."

Ruth felt startled. *How close had she come? And still how close was she to that abyss?*

"What changed you?"

"I don't know. It was in the office. Maybe your fire. A star has to have guts—something more than a body. There are too many bodies willing to strip themselves naked...the offerings are so often and so cheap that...well, as you can see, I have a special room for such activity. Oh, I don't 'use' and 'throw aside,' coldly and brutally. Not *that* simple. Do it that way and you're on the blacklist with agents and promoters. I give the girl some part—something small and unimportant. A walk-on. She gets her sex-worth out of it. That's all they're good for. It's a trap most women fall into. What else can they do? After all, the men in control can push anybody with a little talent and guts to stay with it, and a body, into the spot-light. Look at the Hollywood stars that are big money-makers. They aren't so great! Where are our future greats? Anywhere you want to get them—get them from the gutter, if you want. That's why women have to put out to get ahead. That's why a girl with a lot of talent and good looks, who turns the cold shoulder, won't get past the casting office. Unless she has a lot of money behind her. And where will she get the money? A husband? A father? A mother? A rich uncle? Or a lover? Maybe it's not fair, but—" He broke off, grinning almost boyishly. "Why the hell am I telling you all this?"

"I was wondering that, myself," Ruth admitted, warmly, "Maybe it's a line you give to all the girls you bring up here. How do I know?"

"You don't!" he laughed, almost relieved. "But, you'll find out. You'll find out!" Carlton studied her for a long time, and then he leaned forward, looking at the far wall, supporting his chin on his hands. "It'll take time and pushing and a lot of work. Even if you *can* act worth a damn! It won't be easy and it won't be fun. We'll have to put you in a cheapie. And let the American public take a good look at you, for the first time. Something startling. Maybe a bath, naked. Maybe something startling, like the way you walk across the room." He looked at her, then said: "Stand. Walk across the room!"

"What?"

"Stand! Walk across the room!" he demanded in an impersonal voice. "Do as I tell you!" Anger edged his last words.

"You're kidding?" She couldn't believe him. This new event took several moments for her brain to adjust to.

"Stand! Damn you!" Carlton shouted, standing. Then slowly his face relaxed. "I'm sorry. You'll have to get used to my being like this. When I'm working—well, I get distant."

"You call *this* work?" Ruth asked, slowly standing.

"No! No! It wasn't supposed to be. But, well, you got me thinking—and...well, what I want you to do is to slowly walk across the room. Do it naturally."

Still puzzled, more from the unexpectedness of what was happening, than the event itself, Ruth started across the room.

"Okay—now try it with a little more sex in it!"

"What?"

"Wiggle a little."

Ruth started back toward him, wiggling.

"Oh, come on! Christ! Can't you do better than that? You *have* to do better than that. That's *nothing!* That's no good. Do it more—well, think about the most desirable man you know. Think about how it is to be held in his arms—think about being kissed. Hell, think about the sex act with him. How does it make you feel? Now try doing it again. Walk across the room—as if you were having sexual intercourse!"

Ruth tried again, this time thinking about all the men she had had in the past—all the ones who had been good and exciting. She thought about the feel of their hands on her body, their lips on her breasts, their hips against hers. Mentally she pictured all the by-ways of passion, all the intrigues that two bodies could enjoy together. And the emotion that was conjured up caused her body to take on a new texture, a new rhythm, a new movement.

"Yes—that's good. That's good. You look like you're almost having an orgasm. That's good. Good. Very good."

Ruth turned toward the man. Carlton's face was

lighted with excitement, but of a kind she had never seen in a man's eyes before. There was nothing sexual about his excitement. He was off in a world of dreams, hardly noticing her.

"Well—what's that prove?" Ruth inquired, slapping her fists on her hips.

Carlton's face relaxed, his eyes focused on her body. "It proves there's an animal awareness about you that most women don't have. It tells me why I decided there was something about you deserving more than a quick lay and a walk-on part. It shows that what I saw last night wasn't imagination, but vision. You could become a great star—if you are handled right, if you work hard, and if you do what you're told. It won't be fun. It won't be private, either. You'll have to change your name, and you'll have to change your personality to suit the screen image we'll develop for you. There's no limit to how far you might go, it'll all depend on you and how you're handled. But don't think that's so unusual. It's just that you happen to have it—and its something I've been looking for. Animal sexual awareness. A maturity of experience in a youthful face. How many young women have *that!* Most of the young ones are nothing more than 'Gidgets' and 'Tammys'! You'll be sexsational! Youth—without childishness. You can pass as a mature, experienced woman of thirty—if necessary—or a young, tramp. And you'll stay youthful for a long time—which means a longer time at top—and more money for your backers."

"Why me?" she asked coldly.

"Why you? Because you happened along at the right time at the right place. You clicked. Nothing more. I'm small-time—but you could be big-time. With my help you'll go to the top. I know the business—and I know where the money is. All you have to do is what Davis has been having you do in the past. Please the right people, at the right time. But it doesn't have to be the bed-routine, *all the time.* Money is interested in making money. If you have something to offer, and are presented by the right person to the right people, you don't have to go to bed...Hell, this *calls* for a celebration!" He flung his hands in the air.

Ruth watched as the man drained his scotch and poured himself another.

"How about me?" she asked, finishing off her own drink.

"Sure—sure—sure. Help yourself."

She helped herself. Then they stood there staring at each other. "I don't get you, Carl."

"There's nothing to get. You just happened to be one of the lucky ones. Timing and Timing. That's what counts. You connected. Don't ask me why. There's no reason for it. Unless you call it a sixth sense. In any case, I believe we could go places with you. I believe there's money in your body—if promoted correctly. And...I want money."

"And—sex?" She indicated the bed. "Wasn't that what we came up here for?"

The man frowned, puzzled. "Yes. That is what we came up here for, isn't it?" But his voice didn't sound so sure; it was distant; his eyes were glassy.

"You mean that—"

"That I'd let it stay here—with no intimacy?"

"Well?" She raised her shoulders in question.

"You still have the strange, childish idea that

sex is your own key to success. That just isn't so. Whether we sleep together or not has nothing to do with what I'll do for you—or with you."

Ruth smiled. "But...there's nothing saying that you can't have what we came up here for. Regardless." Her voice was husky, but honestly so, and her tone intimate and inviting.

They moved to the bed and sat down, sipping their drinks in silence, as if waiting for the right moment.

This was something new to Ruth, and for the first time in her life she felt a sense of awkwardness with a man. Before, all her relationships had been brutally crude, a case of undressing and presenting herself to the man, fast and simple. No build-ups.

Oh, there had been a few men who had taken their time, she had to admit, *but nothing like this!*

The soft music was slowly doing its work, slowly building the mood. It seemed to Ruth as if she were with a man that she loved. There was no fooling herself that there could be any emotion between the two of them, yet a strange awareness settled over her; a feeling of romance. It was as if they were playing out a scene in a movie. And, in a way, she realized, this was exactly what they were doing. The setting was Movieland itself, romantic music, cocktails, beautiful bedroom.

The man's hand crept around her shoulder and circled her body, the fingers caressing softly into one supple breast. Carlton moved his lips closer and she could feel the warmth of his breath against her flesh.

"Ruth—you're a very beautiful woman," he breathed into her ear.

His fingers tensed slightly, drawing Ruth closer. Then suddenly his lips brushed her cheek and she turned, meeting them with her own.

A welling passion, a terrible need, she hadn't ever felt before, overwhelmed her. It was more than physical; it was more than emotional. It was perfection. A demanding force moved her. All created by the room, the music and this man.

Their kisses blended. Their tongues met, hungrily. Suddenly she was lying back on the bed, the man bending over her, his hands caressing across her body, his lips buried into the white creamy hollow of her throat, his breath hot against her flesh.

A mixture of emotions drowned over Ruth. She felt amazement that all this was happening, amazement that it had happened so fast, so unexpectedly, so differently than she would have thought possible. This was her big moment, her big chance—her big contact. And it was more than that! The man's hands were caressing aside the clothing off her body, whispering over the softness of her white flesh, building wild, intense desire. She stopped thinking logically.

Her mind was spinning from the events of the evening, from the effects of the liquor and the effects of the man's caressing hands and lips. He kissed her body as if it were some delightful feast of which he could never tire. Ruth found herself going wildly insane with wanting; a wanting she'd never before felt for a man. This was something very special, in a way she couldn't understand, and wasn't able to even try to understand, at that moment. If it was illusion, it was lovely. That far she could willingly embrace. Soft, velvet, romantic illusion.

Ruth clawed at the man with every nerve in her body.. She felt him drive down at her with a gentle force and then felt pleasure attacked her nerves. There was the sound of gasps, moans, of sighs, and it wasn't a long time before Ruth realized they came from her own throat.

Then, finally, the world burst and all that was left was pure perfection of physical sensation. Slowly it ebbed away, leaving her exhausted, spent out, for the first time in her life, totally satisfied. Awareness stayed for only a short while, then it faded and darkness closed over her mind.

CHAPTER FIVE

The next morning Ruth returned to Davis' apartment, but a sense of irritation settled over her. John was still asleep. Ruth had already made up her mind about one thing: she would have to get an apartment of her own.

The long six months with John Davis had held its bright moments; but now was the time to end all this and bring a finish to her relations with the man. He was a part of her past. Carlton Turner was her immediate future.

Ruth sat in the living room for a long time, thinking about Carlton Turner, and all the things he had promised her.

She lighted a cigarette, taking a deep drag.

Her mind was still spinning from the events of the last hours. A lot had happened. A lot more than she would have thought possible. The day before yesterday had been an agony of waiting for that moment when she'd meet the "Big Man". Now that the fact was a part of her life, and the beginning step to a Hollywood career, she dreaded the scene that would have to be played out with John Davis.

She put out her cigarette, stood, stepped to the window and looked out over the city.

There had been long months with John Davis,

and she couldn't help feeling a sense of affection for the man. It wasn't possible to live with another person for such a long time without feeling some emotional attachment. But one thing she'd learned: when people, events or places became useless to her, it was necessary to leave them.

Turner was her new mark—and she'd use him as long as it was profitable.

Sighing, Ruth turned and walked across the room, into the hallway and then opened the bedroom door.

Davis was lying in bed, the covers half off his body.

"John! John!" Ruth called, shaking his shoulder. Slowly the man stirred, then sat up in bed "Hey—what's going on?"

"Get up! It's time we talked."

"What about?" he asked, sleepily. Then his mind seemed to clear and he grinned up at her. "Pulled it off?"

"Better than you think!"

A frown crinkled his forehead. "What's that mean?"

"I don't know how to tell you this—but I believe the direct, honest, approach might be best."

"What you talking about?" He was fully awake, glaring at her.

"I'm moving out."

"What?"

"We agreed, right from the beginning—no strings attached!—I'd move when I wanted to. That was the deal—and I'm leaving!"

For a moment the man glared at her and slowly he moved from the bed. "You can't do that, honey.

You should know me better than that!"

"Don't threaten me, John. A deal's a deal. You got your money's worth out of me. Free lays—and pimping-money!"

The man's face drew white. He leaned forward, every muscle tensing. "Let's not make a scene, Ruthie..."

"John, it's over."

"Dumping me?" Anger was slowly replacing sleepiness.

"That's about the size of it."

"Why? Got yourself another playmate?" he demanded, nastily.

"Let's just say I've outgrown you, that's all." Suddenly she was enjoying herself. Memory of how she had been used, how she'd been forced into doing the dirty film, and the way he'd made deals behind her back, caused pleasure to rush through her. "I heard about your little deal—with Baker and Carlton."

"So what? You didn't expect me to play for nothing, did you? What can you do about it?"

"I've done it. Carlton is backing me—*me,* personally—without *you!*" She laughed at his face. A feeling of hate welled up in her. "You tried to 'take' me—and got 'took' instead."

John grinned back. "You forget the party film."

Silence fell on the room. For a long time Ruth couldn't think of anything to say. Finally the words formed on her lips: "What are you talking about?"

"I think you'll play along with me. A private contract. Money. On the side. A percentage of the take. For yours truly. You can move out, and all that. I expected something like this, in the long run.

But you'll be making a mistake doing it now. You don't think you're the first girl Carlton has conned into bed, do you?"

"Don't take me for a sucker, John. The deal was made, with or without the bed-routine."

He looked surprised, but recovered quickly.

"The little film you made is my insurance that I'll be cut in on a piece of you—in any case." He looked triumphant.

"And...if I don't play along?"

"Your imagination should fill in the details. What do you think a film like that would do to your so-called 'big' dreams?"

A sickening grind ran down her back. "You wouldn't—"

"Don't kid yourself, honey. I'd sell my mother to the devil, if I thought it'd bring a little fast buck to yours truly! Don't play the innocent with me. You might think you're pretty smart, suckering the marks—but you forgot one thing: we're from the same gutter—and I know a few tricks. I've been in the gutter a little longer than you have. So don't try playing innocent!"

"You *are* a real bastard, aren't you?" Ruth stated, numbed with shock.

"And you're a whoring bitch, and when you forget that, you—"

Ruth's hand lashed across his face.

John glared at her. Then, without warning, his hand slapped back, connecting at the side of her face, jarring her head to one side. For a moment she stood there, stunned. Then gasping for breath, she turned on the man, like a savage animal. A scream broke from her bleeding lips.

Ruth's hands swung claw-like, the nails scraping flesh from the man's face. It was like swinging through a red haze. Nothing mattered, nothing was important except getting back at this brute who had dared to hit her.

"Goddamn!" John Davis cursed.

Then something slammed at the point of her chin, jarring her whole head with the force of its impact. Never in her life had she felt such agonized pain. It seemed as if she had been lifted several yards into the air, spun around and smashed against a wall. The back of her skull hit something hard, and then blackness exploded into being.

* * * * * * *

John Davis was returning from the bathroom with a damp rag to revive her, when she came to. He leaned over Ruth, concern heavy on his face.

"God, I'm sorry," he managed to choke out.

The numbness slowly ebbed away as the man put a cold compress on her jaw. "I've never done a thing like I that—"

"Forget it!" she moaned, struggling to her feet.

"I mean it, Ruth. I'm sorry about this. You threw me a curve. I wasn't expecting it. I thought things were pretty solid between us."

"Yeah!" Bitterness was tight inside her throat. John's sudden change was unnerving.

"Look—forget what I said," he pleaded.

"What?"

"I'm sorry. So, I'm busted out—so, you go on by yourself. You were right—I got something out of the deal. Let's leave it there. I'll take care of Baker."

Ruth stared at him, amazed. It wasn't like John to be that way.

"What's gotten into you?" she questioned, her voice shaking.

"I don't know. Just that...hell, I guess I cared more about you than I realized." He hesitated, stepping away from her. His face revealed the amazement that his own words must have caused him to feel. "I...well, for what it's worth, I guess you've grown to mean something more to me than I would have thought possible—well, in any case—I've acted like a bastard. Don't ask me why—but I'll help you."

Ruth guessed the truth, even though it was fantastic:

John loved her in his own way, but was afraid to admit it even to himself.

"It's not like you, John," she pointed out, gently.

"Hell, don't you think I know it? It's been me against the world. I've conned everything and everybody—all my life. I've taken like a hungry animal, anything I could get. And—I don't know why—but when—well, I hit you—I suddenly felt sick. All at once I realized what...what you meant to me. Damn!" He hesitated, his face contorting savagely. Then after a moment he continued, more calmly, more impersonally:

"I guess it's something about you—something I saw, and others have seen in you. Some women are just sluts—press a button and they spread their legs—tramps! And then there are other—damned few, luckily for us men—who have an element about them that causes men to do things they wouldn't do otherwise. You've got it. And if you

86

use it right—well, you'll go a long way."

"That's quite a speech."

"No conning, this time. I meant it. You have money?"

"I saved a little. Enough to see me through."

"If you ever need it—look me up. I made enough off you. And if you need a friend—I'll make up for what I did just now...I'll never forgive myself for that!"

Ruth felt emotion burst within her and threw herself into his arms, sobbing. It was the first time she'd felt that way about anybody except her father. All her life had been a struggle against the male sex. She'd never really built a friendship with a man.

"Hey—stop that, girl!" John scolded, holding her head up "Don't start things like that. You should be happy. If Carlton means it—he'll probably do a lot more than I did. Just don't forget I'm a friend—for what I'm worth."

"Why?" Tears streamed down her cheeks.

"Maybe because we're pretty much the same kind. In any case, I like you a damned lot. You—well, I never gave much thought about how I felt about you—but that's past. In any case, it's been a strange relationship. Pick up a broad at a bar—have her about the place for a spell. What ever in the world made me offer the apartment? I've puzzled over that one for months. It didn't make sense. But . . you have a magic, Ruth—use it right—and get on top." Gently he pushed her away. "We *did* have a ball, didn't we?"

Ruth nodded. "Considering you were pimping for me—yeah. I should hate you!"

"I guess you should," he admitted.

"Damned if I don't think you're embarrassed!" she exploded, laughing. "Hell, you only did what I wanted you to do. We had a good partnership, didn't we?"

They were silent for a long time, staring at each other.

Finally she shrugged, and said, "Well, I guess I might as well pack my things and start looking for some place to live."

John's face drew tight, but he said nothing as he helped her pack the belongings she'd gathered since living with him.

* * * * * *

That evening she had settled herself in a small single on Yucca Street, one block north of Hollywood Boulevard. It was a cozy, warm place with a large kitchen. The living room had a studio couch that opened up into a double bed. Ruth felt a sense of excitement about her future. John had driven her around Hollywood until she had found this furnished apartment. He bought a bottle and then they had a good-bye drink. Much to her surprise, John hadn't attempted a pass. She had expected it and planned to let him have her. But it would have been wrong to let John make love to her. It was over, and he'd had enough sense to realize it.

Strange, she thought, *how things had happened.*

She was just a small town girl, raised on a farm, who had discovered the by-ways of sex at a much too early age. She had used her body through her teen-age, and when she was eighteen, left home, gone to Kansas City, gotten a job as a waitress, shared a small apartment with another young woman, and settled down to a short, but revealing experience, which had taught her some of the facts of life.

Ruth's roommate had turned out to be bisexual, and had made several attempts to seduce her. That was where she had drawn the line. Not that the idea of relations with a woman seemed wrong or dirty. It was just that there had seemed no point in relations with a woman when she could so easily have a man. Her attitude had been: why take hamburger when she could have steak. The restaurant job had given her plenty of chances to meet men. After a couple of months with a roommate, Ruth had decided it was far better to have a place of her own. She rented a small one bedroom apartment, into which a lot of men had finally passed. During this time she had learned that men would pay more than just a bottle of booze and a hotel room for the night's games. One night a man she'd picked up had pointed out that he could get her real hard cash for what she was putting out for free. He knew men in town who would pay a lot for her services. He turned out to be a contact man and had taught her most of what she knew about prostitution and the call-girl racket. There had developed a profitable relationship between them. Within a week, after starting to sleep for money, Ruth had quit her job at the restaurant and taken up full time prostitution.

Ruth suddenly found her thoughts turning to Carlton Turner.

His love-making had been different. It was a mixture of tenderness and passion. Davis had been tender—but there had never been any fooling about what was happening: they were sexing it for sex sake. With Carlton, Ruth could almost believe it was something more.

Imagination brought to full power by the romantic setting? her mind questioned. But it was something wonderful she would never forget. Carlton was the first man who had really meant anything more than a quick bed session. And that was important! He was romantic!

The next day she was supposed to call Carlton at his office.

Ruth downed her drink and poured another, pulled out the studio couch and started making the bed. A little later she was lying under the covers, smoking, sipping whiskey. A long time later, Ruth turned out the light and lay back, letting sleep overcome her exhausted body.

CHAPTER SIX

The next day when Ruth called Carlton's office she received a numbing shock.

"Yes?" inquired the secretary, impersonally.

"This is Ruth Browne, Mr. Carlton asked me to call him today." She felt excitement flow through every nerve.

"I'll see if he's in."

There was a long silence. Then finally the secretary said: "I'm sorry, but he's busy."

"Well, when will he be free?" Ruth inquired.

"I don't know. If you'll leave your phone number...I'm sure he'll call you when he has time."

"I don't have any phone!"

"I'm sorry, I can't do anything for you."

"What's the meaning of this?" Anger flushing her cheeks. "I want to talk to Carl, right away!"

"Mr. Turner is in conference and said he couldn't be bothered," the woman's voice announced.

"He said—"

"He said that he was terribly busy and to get your phone number. He'd call you as soon as he had time."

"You tell him he can—" Ruth broke off. She was just about to tell the woman that Carlton could go to hell and back, but decided against it. Slowly she hung up.

Ruth suddenly felt lonely; helpless. Had he really been giving her a line? Had he just pulled a fast one.

She stepped out of the phone booth. Her knees were weak and sweat was breaking out over her body. Her throat was dry and felt the sudden need for a drink. She stepped into a bar and ordered a double Martini. After a second cocktail, Ruth felt a little better; but madder.

Nobody was going to double-cross her—no matter who it might be—or how little and unimportant they thought she was. You're Ruth Browne—and you know your way around the world!

Ruth hurried out of the bar. She found a phone booth and looked in the phone book. Ruth found *Carlton Studios,* jotted down the address and then called for a cab. Thirty minutes later she was stepping into the office just south of Melrose. She felt a sense of disappointment, having believed that Carlton Turner would have a more plush office. But she shrugged off the depression and stepped up to the small window through which she could see a telephone operator.

"I'd like to talk to Carlton Turner!" she demanded. The woman looked up, smiled, asked: "What's your name?"

"Ruth Browne!"

"I'll see if he's in."

The woman picked up a phone, said there was a Miss Browne wanted to see Mr. Turner. After a silence, she turned and looked up at Ruth. "I'm sorry—but he's not in right now."

There wasn't anything she could do.

Ruth slowly turned and walked out of the office.

There were other ways to get hold of Carlton Turner, told herself.

* * * * * * *

It had been dark for hours, and no movement or sign of life had revealed itself inside Carlton Turner's large Beverly Hills home. The place was dead silent, black.

Ruth had been waiting for well over three hours. She was tired, exhausted and sick. Emotions had ripped up through her whole body, each minute making them more violent. Then, as the fourth hour slipped by, she realized how foolish all this was.

"You have to admit, Ruth, that maybe he *was* busy, today. Maybe you should give him another chance," she said out loud to herself.

The thought of calling John Davis flashed through her mind, but she pushed it aside. The less she had to do with the man the better it would be. She'd taken Carlton's word that he would help her, and possibly he meant it. If not, she could turn to Davis; start all over. That thought annoyed her. Ruth started walking away from Carlton's home, continued until she came to a phone booth. She called for a cab, and when it arrived, gave the cabby her address. Once home she fixed herself a drink. The first drink numbed the emotional reaction. More drinks followed until she was unconscious.

* * * * * * *

The next day it was the same story.

They were sorry, but Mr. Turner was busy. If she would like to leave her phone number, they would call her.

Ruth got drunk that evening. She sat alone in her apartment until the liquor blurred all thoughts; all those tormenting mental agonies that threatened her emotional sanity.

When she awoke the next morning, a throbbing hangover was pounding at her temples.

A shower and a breakfast of fried eggs helped to clear away the pain. After a cup of coffee she left the apartment and went to the corner phone booth and gave her name and asked to speak to Mr. Turner. After a moment another woman's voice said:

"Hello, is this Miss Ruth Browne?"

"Yes?" Her heart jumped.

"Mr. Turner left a message that if you called again to give you his home number."

"Isn't he in?" Ruth inquired, disappointed.

"Not right now. But he said that you'd stand a better chance of getting him at home. He seemed to feel it important...if you'll take it, you might get him, now. I doubt if he has left for the office, yet."

Ruth took the number. She placed money into the change box and dialed. Held her breath.

A maid answered.

"Could I speak to Mr. Turner."

"Who's calling?" the maid inquired.

"Ruth Browne. His office told me to call."

There was a moment's hesitation and then the maid said: "I'll see if he's up. Would you please wait a moment?"

Ruth waited. It seemed forever. Not until now had the full effect of what had happened really startled through her. Now she suddenly felt foolish about how she'd acted in his office.

A sleepy male voice came from the receiver.

"Hello, Ruth, Carl."

Ruth gasped, sucked in her breath and counted hurriedly to ten, trying to gain control of her pounding heart.

"Ruth—are you there?"

"Yes. Yes."

"You had me worried. I'm sorry about the office. Things have been pretty wild these last few days. But that's past. Can you come over—in an hour?"

"Yes," Ruth answered in a shaky voice. Before she realized it, the phone line was dead.

* * * * * * *

Carlton was dressed in a silken brown robe, pulled tightly around his large body. He sat at the table, idly playing with a breakfast steak. There was a half finished Scotch and Soda beside his plate and a cup of black coffee on the other side. So far the only thing that had been exchanged between them was polite greetings and his apology for still eating breakfast. He'd offered her a drink, which she'd accepted. The maid was in the kitchen.

"I guess you think I was playing around," Carlton observed, looking up at Ruth.

"I *was* a little surprised by the brush-off the office gave me," Ruth admitted candidly. "A little mad, too."

95

"I heard about that yesterday. That's why I told them to give you my home phone. Enough is enough. I'm really sorry about that. But, as I told you, things are pretty heavy."

He was silent for a long while, finishing off his steak. He gulped down his scotch when the maid came in. "Give me another," he instructed.

"Guess you're wondering what'll happen next," Carlton said.

"Yes."

"Well, don't." He was thoughtful for a moment, then added: "It'll take time. But I think we can write a walk-on for you in this movie I'm doing now. A quick couple of minutes. But it has to be just right. Not a maid bit—not a bit—*period!* It has to have some snap. Something that will knock the John Q. Public on its ears. Get attention. Then we'll play up the publicity end." The man's eyes paused at the full creamy bulge of her breasts, that were revealed in the dipping neckline of her pink dress. "When can you move in here?"

"What?" Ruth tensed, surprised. She stared at him, unable to adjust to his sudden change of subject.

"When can you move in here?" he repeated, his voice heavy with irritation. "It's a simple question!"

"I didn't know—"

"Oh, come on! Don't play the child."

Ruth recovered. "So that's it?"

"Part of it! Not *all* of it!"

"Okay—give me the works. Fill me in on *all* the details. You seem to have worked things out without consulting me! And I don't like surprises." she snapped, angered.

96

"You move in here, with me. It'll make things easier. You'll need a lot of work done—a lot of training—a lot of...*everything!* I'll have to put a lot of time in you—and we can't be playing the cozy routine of driving back and forth between my place and yours. It has little to do with what you seem to think. Sure, I'll make use of your personal ser-vices...no man would turn that down. You'll have your own room, and when you're not busy working on developing your new 'personality' you'll be given little duties to do—to help pay for your keep. When I want to go to bed with you—you'll be here, waiting for me."

"I didn't think you were going to give roses, free of charge—but I didn't believe you'd be so pointed about it!" Ruth admonished.

"Oh, hell! Don't pull that virgin crap on me. You're a tramp with a good body and a lot of guts. And—" The maid came with his drink; he was silent until she had left.

"And we're both past the stage of considering any holding hands relationship. So why play games? I had you pegged from the beginning. I don't want any misunderstandings between us. You'll serve as my mistress when I want you. You don't interfere with my personal life—I take what I want—and you get what you can out of me. You'll get a big start in movies. You'll do what I tell you—do it *when* I tell you and the *way* I tell you!" His eyes burned mean-ingfully into hers. "Do you understand?"

Ruth gulped down the scotch, holding back the fury inside her. If Carlton Turner was going to push her into Stardom, there was no reason in the world why he shouldn't demand the use of her body. That was business. Maybe he could have been more subtle and gentle; but it was his right to say it any way he wished to. He held the cards. Ruth realized what shocked her was the complete reversal from the other evening. Then, it had been romantic—now, it was brutal, daylight business. A deal. A pact. Nothing more. He wanted to help her into a career; and wanted the complete and exclusive use of her body, in return.

If that's the way he wanted to play it, then he'd have it that way.

But, for some reason she felt hurt.

"Okay, Carl—it's a deal."

"I thought so!" he exclaimed, grinning. Then his hand reached out and affectionately touched hers. "You're okay, Ruthie. You're okay. I think we'll have a ball, from now on. You'll have to excuse the cold brashness of my approach—I didn't want to make it easy for you. From now on it'll be wine and roses—and some goddamned hard work!"

PART III

CHAPTER SEVEN

Three months of lovely, wonderful hell had slowly passed. Ruth's first scene in a small unimportant movie had been finally finished.

Ruth looked around the small, expensive cocktail lounge, and then returned her attention to the drink in front of her.

How many more will you have to drink before Mister Big decides to arrive? she wondered, vaguely annoyed.

The long day at the studio had drained her nerves. She was glad that the shooting was finally over. It had been a long, hard struggle. As she sipped her third drink, Ruth thought back over the three months that had climaxed with this day's work.

Carlton had been a mixture of a demon and a romantic. He was a hard, demanding man; a wonderful lover; a selfish bastard.

But the days and weeks had held a magical charm. Even during the work she had found an excitement that had made it possible to stand Carlton's everlasting badgering.

"Walk across the room," the man had shouted over and over again. "Do it like you were in bed with a man! No! That's not right! More sex in it!

Come on now, Ruth. Damn it all, you can do it! You've done it before..."

How many days had that gone on? She had lost count. Then there was the routine of learning her "real-life" personality.

"Now, let's run through the lines...when a reporter asks you what you think about sex, what do you say?"

"It's here to stay!"

"More sex in your voice. Say it again!"

Then the other questions: "What do you wear to bed?"

Nothing!

"Do you have a boy friend?"

Yes!

"Care to name him?"

All of them?

"What is the woman's place in the home?"

The bedroom, don't you think?

Silly questions and silly answers, Ruth thought angrily. But it was meant to project an image of raw sex appeal, free and wild, savage and willing

That was the work, but not the life. Living in the big house with Carlton, Ruth had acquired a taste for its luxuries, its money and class. She had learned how to act in social company, how to project a sexual awareness, without being awkward or crude about it She had learned what it was to be a "Big Star", by seeing other big stars. But most of all, she had learned what it was like to live with Carlton Turner. There were moments of extreme brutality, when he didn't want to be bothered, or when he was busy working on something else, or when he was giving her instructions. But his moments of tenderness and love—they were something completely different.

Yes, Ruth thought, *it was fun living with Carlton Turner. He was a good lover, tender and thoughtful.*

Those nights in the Romancing Room, as she called it, had helped to keep her in a continued state of emotional excitement toward Carlton. It wasn't love, for Ruth didn't fool herself about that emotion; but it was affection and need and wanting. It was like being filled for the first time, when there had been only emptiness before. His lips would move over her body like no other man's lips ever had. His hands would search across her naked flesh like hot fire. It was these wild moments in his arms that had made it possible for her to take all the cruelty his instructions and direction had rained upon her.

She looked at the diamond-studded watch Carlton had given her. It was 9:30. He was already an hour late.

The waitress placed another Martini before her. She was finishing the drink when Carlton's voice interrupted her thoughts.

Carlton was standing in front of her. At his side was a young man.

"Sorry about being late, honey, but this joker here—well, it all turned up unexpectedly." Carlton sat opposite Ruth; the young man slid into the booth next to her.

"Ruth—this is Jimmy Belmont—I guess you've heard about him. A big recording star," Carlton introduced.

"So?" Ruth inquired, turning her attention to the young man. He was just a boy. Their eyes met and his were questioning, probing; subtle interest was alive in his expression. She politely nodded.

"Hello, Miss Browne." The man was grinning like a teenager.

With a sense of irritation, Ruth rejected him as dullsville. She looked at Carlton. "Okay, so what's the pitch?"

Nervously she fingered her half empty martini glass.

"I want the two of you to become friends."

Ruth didn't miss the implication in his voice.

"Okay, Carl—spell it out for me," she demanded coldly, ignoring the young man next to her.

"You need a little publicity. Jimmy here is interested in publicity. We're planning a picture for Jimmy—and thinking of starring you in it, opposite him," Carlton explained. "First a little scandal—a romance—and then the picture."

Ruth felt jarred by the coldness of the man's announcement. His voice was a low whisper, direct and without emotion. She looked around the room, realizing how impossible it would be to blast into a scene with Carlton. She couldn't help smiling inwardly; the man had arranged things to crunch down her temper. Carlton knew people—and he seemed to know her inside out.

"Don't you think this is a little sudden?" Ruth inquired.

"Nothing's sudden in this business, Ruthie— you might as well get used to it. We've made our point with the film. In a couple of months you'll be getting a lot of publicity. We want you seen in public with Jimmy, *before* the film comes out! We want the little wagging tongues saying nasty things about the two of you. We want a play on sex. You're going to be a sex symbol—if we're able to push you that far. We'll need something big to do it. You'll flaunt sex all over the place. You start *here!*" Carlton stood, still grinning. "Have fun, kids!"

Without another word he turned and walked out of the lounge.

There was a long dead silence. Ruth finished off her drink and then turned and looked at her new date.

Jimmy Belmont had boyish features, thick full lips, and a thin, soft looking body. His eyes were almost childishly innocent looking.

"So—he wants us to do the bed routine?" Ruth announced coldly, looking directly into his eyes, hoping to shock him with the blatant remark.

Jimmy turned away.

"Wouldn't put it that way, Miss," he said in a low voice.

"How *would* you put it, *boy?*" she inquired nastily. Jimmy jerked around, staring at her. "Look, Miss—Browne—you can cut the jazzy talk. You aren't talking to a hick. I got the world in my hands!" His face contorted ugly, his hand squeezed together into a tight fist in front of her eyes. "You're a nothing! A nothing! I can split you in two. Don't try anything jazzy with me!"

Ruth held down her surprised anger. She now looked at him more closely. There were light, subtle lines around his dark brown eyes; and the corners of his mouth had a mature look she hadn't noticed before. She began to wonder about his age.

"Okay—I'm sorry. Carl pulled a fast one. I thought he was my date, tonight. I'd been waiting for over an hour. That's not good for a woman's temper." She forced the corners of her full lips upwards into a smile.

"So—you got busted!" His voice was less emotional. He looked at her for a long time without saying anything. "You know—you're more attractive than your photo. I thought you'd be a ball—from what Mr. Turner told me—but I didn't know you'd be so—well, damn it all, you have sex written all over you." His eyes dropped to her dipping neckline.

"I guess it's not your fault," Ruth offered, politely. It didn't really make much difference who shared her bed, as long as the man knew what he was doing. Even then she'd been with some pretty awkward guys; maybe it wouldn't be so bad with this Jimmy Belmont.

"Mr. Turner is really pushing for you—Ruth. I guess I can call you that. In any case—he thinks you'll go places; thinks the two of us in a film together would be good box-office."

Ruth shrugged. "I guess he knows what he's doing." She hesitated; then asked: "Where, now?"

"Where do you want to go? Carlton is footing the bill."

Ruth considered and then smiled inwardly.

Well, she thought, *if that's the way it was, there wasn't any reason why they couldn't have a blast-oft. Really make the bastard pay through the nose.*

"Everywhere!" she exploded. "We might as well make the most of it!"

* * * * * * *

They began at one of the large Hollywood Steak

Houses that features thick steaks, with large baked potatoes, sour cream and chives. Cocktails were served before and during the meal. Afterwards Jimmy suggested a night club that was featuring a singer friend of his. Drinks, music, dancing and the show, followed one after another.

The feel of Jimmy Belmont's body against hers, made Ruth dizzy with physical need. He was hard and solid under the jet black suit. That surprised her. Another thing surprised Ruth was the fact that Jimmy was a good conversationalist. They had covered the international political situations, the music scene, the problems with Cuba, and the space program. The man had a dry, quiet wit. It was almost possible to forget the dirty trick Carlton had pulled on her; it was almost possible to forget that they were out together by direct orders of the studio.

Amazingly, she found herself enjoying the date.

The drinks helped. Martini followed Martini. The fact that she didn't fall on her face, surprised Ruth. It was the first time for months that she'd had an all-out spree. With Carlton it had been hard work, with a few romantic evenings at home; but nothing as wild as this evening.

In fact, she realized, as they settled down into a small booth in an intimate hotel club, *she had never been on such a fling before in her life.*

Ruth looked across the small table at her escort. His face seemed to have matured during the evening. But she realized this was merely her own mental attitude toward him. At the beginning she'd rejected the idea of spending the night with him. Now she reconsidered.

"What time is it?" Ruth inquired.

"A little after one. Things are closing down. That's the trouble with L.A. Everything's dead after two. Back East you can ball it up all night—and stagger home, like a zombie, in the morning." He smiled, reaching for her hand. "I'll admit I didn't like the set-up, at first. My agent and Carlton made the arrangements. I was pushed into it, just like you. Didn't want to admit it, at the beginning. We hit off pretty bad, didn't we?"

Ruth nodded, pleased.

"It's been fun," she agreed, softly. "At least we can thank them for making a good match."

Jimmy nodded. "You thought of me as a little squirt, didn't you?"

Ruth considered and then finally said: "Yes. How old are you?"

"Twenty-nine."

"You're kidding?"

"Twenty-one for public—but...afraid I've been knocking around for a long time. Was in the service some years back—that's when I decided to make the show-business routine. Boy! What some kids will do! I thought it'd be a snap!"

"Wasn't it?" Ruth inquired. "Seems I've heard about you—your name sounded...well I'm sure I've read it some place."

"Thanks for nothing." He grinned. "It's worked out, slowly. But I'm one of the top singers now— and still climbing."

"Not modest about it?"

"Should I be?"

"I guess not."

Drinks came. Ruth was glad, because the liquor had worn off, leaving her sleepy; a condition that

108

was not desirable for what she now had in mind.

"It still seems early," Ruth pointed out, taking a sip of her Black Russian.

"It's early. In any hurry to go home?"

"Home is where you sleep...that depends," was her counter remark.

A gleam flashed in the man's eyes. "Is that supposed to mean something?"

"Take it or leave it, any way you want," she challenged, moistening the surface of her lips with the point of her tongue.

He grinned, but didn't say anything.

They sipped their drinks for a long time. The silence seemed weighted and awkward. Ruth finally decided to plunge direct to the point.

"This is a nice hotel, isn't it?"

"Yeah. Nice. Good place to stay."

Ruth laughed. She couldn't help herself. Here was sitting a teenage idol, a man who claimed to have been around; and he was fumbling the ball. There was more than five years difference between their ages, and yet he was nervous and awkward in his attempts to get her into a hotel room. There wasn't any doubt in her mind that the seed had been planted; but the man was unsure of himself.

"Okay, Jimmy. I know what you have in mind. I have the same thought. Why don't we stay here. After all, that's what Carl would want. The SOB!" That last she'd said in a low whisper, half to herself. "Well, anyway—why not? You're a boy and I'm a girl and..."

"You didn't look like the type that would."

"Oh, come on, Jimmy. Don't play the innocent with me. I might look young—but between you and me—I've probably had more experience than you have."

His eyes hardened and a flush worked his cheeks. "What you know?"

Again Ruth laughed. He had sounded like a foolish kid, wet behind the ears. It amazed her that a man could be so clumsy.

"Let's say I know men. Is that enough?" Their eyes met, challengingly.

"Okay, young lady! Let's go!"

"Calm down, lover. You get the room, I'll finish the drinks!" She had purposely made her voice nasty, demanding, superior.

He glared at her and then stood; he stomped across the small lounge and into the hotel lobby.

Ruth sat there, silently, fighting to control the laughter welling up in her. Maybe it would be fun shocking the *boy*.

That's strange, she thought, finishing her drink, *he's older than you, and you think of him as a boy. But, that's what he is!*

A thrill shot through Ruth at the thought of having a new lover after three months with Carlton. The older man was a good, experienced lover and romancer—but Ruth had never been with one man for so long, and the urge for something different was suddenly exciting. Then another emotion attacked her. She shrugged it off. It was what Turner deserved.

Jimmy returned and said they could go up to the room.

"Order a bottle of booze," she demanded in a coarse voice. "I want a spree, low and dirty!"

* * * * * * *

As the door closed behind them, Ruth looked at the modern room. "A nice place," she observed, reaching to the back of her dress, unzipping it. The cloth slowly edged downwards and finally settled in a ring around her legs. She stepped out of the ring and kicked it aside. She turned to Jimmy, standing before him in bra and panties.

"You think you know something about women? Well, you're about to get yourself a big, fat lesson!" She laughed and quickly slipped out of her bra. Taking a deep breath, she expanded her chest, her breasts thrusting outwards, invitingly; their pink centers were already tightening.

"What the hell!" Jimmy cried, surprised, clutching the bottle of whiskey he'd bought from the bartender down stairs. His eyes grew large as they examined her youthful body.

Ruth merely laughed at him and slipped her fingers under the elastic of her panties. "Like me to take them off?"

The man recovered slightly. He glared at her. "Okay—so you're sexy as hell! And you know you are. And you've been around and aren't shy about being naked in front of a man! That's nothing! What does it prove? I get my share of beautiful broads."

Ruth's mouth opened, started to say something and then slowly compressed.

"Want a drink?" Jimmy inquired, walking into the bathroom and returning with two glasses.

"That's what I wanted the booze for!" she snapped, angry. Ruth stood there in the middle of the room, her fingers tucked under the elastic of her panties. She hadn't moved.

Jimmy poured the water glasses half full and stepped up to her. She took the offered drink. As she was gulping several swallows of whiskey, she felt the man's hand cup under one breast, his fingers flicked over a rigid nipple.

"A hot one, aren't you?" he asked, stepping back.

She was about to say something brutally nasty when she saw the expression on his face. He was smiling, but this time in a friendly manner.

"Don't you think we've been on each other's back long enough for one evening?" he asked.

Ruth relaxed and smiled. "Okay—so I was childish—trying to impress you." Then she added, after taking another swallow of the raw whiskey: "But I was serious about wanting it hard and dirty. I haven't had an old fashioned spree for oven three months. I need it. You just happened along—you're picked. Want it?"

"You kidding? No man would turn you down— if he wanted to call himself a man." He leered at her, then said: "What kind of woman are you?"

"What kind do you think?"

"I don't know." He suddenly seemed more mature, calm. His eyes appraised her in a careful calculating way.

"What kind are you?"

"I'm a tramp. If that's what you want to know. I like sex. I've liked sex ever since the first time. I developed early." She sat down on the bed.

"You have nice legs," Jimmy told her.

"Thanks. Is that all?"

"Breasts, too. I can see why Carlton was interested in you."

"What does *that* mean?" Her question was filled with sharp anger.

"Merely that Carlton goes for good looking broads. But I wasn't sure how far he'd gone with you. Now I know. And I know why he's pushing so hard." Jimmy hesitated and then asked, his voice puzzled: "How can a guy do a thing like that to a woman?"

"What?"

"This! This—what we're doing, now. It's a dirty trick!"

"I guess it is. But that's Carl. He's the bastard type, anyway. Women aren't things with feelings—they're dolls to use; to *be* used. I don't even think he believes I'm human—not in the sense that other people are human."

"Are you?"

"Goddamned yes!"

"Don't you feel resentful about—about this?"

"No. Not really."

"I'd hate his guts, if I were you." Jimmy stood and moved in front of her looking down into her eyes. "You're too lovely to be pushed around from bed to bed."

Ruth started to laugh and then realized he was quite serious. She frowned, wondering why he should care. The mood was completely different from what she'd wanted.

"Don't make a mistake, Jimmy. I'm nothing to most men. I'm a good lay to the ones that know me—nothing more. Carl is helping me—and he's using me, at the same time. It's a cold-blooded business arrangement."

113

A concerned expression clouded the young man's face. "How can a woman be like that?"

"What's different between a woman and a man? Breasts? Certainly not the mind. We both have the same desires. I'm lucky to like sex; so I don't mind being shoved around—it just startled me this evening—plus the fact that I had a hard day of shooting my one and only scene. Nerves. That's all." She raised her head, proudly; her eyes unemotionally level with his.

Silence. Long and awkward.

Finally.

"This isn't much of a spree!" Ruth announced, standing, wiggling herself across the room to where the bottle was sitting on the dresser. She poured whiskey into the glass, went into the bathroom and filled it with water. She returned, looked at the man, downed several swallows of the drink and then lay the glass on the dresser beside the bottle.

"It's about time things got lively!"

Ruth slipped her hands under her panties and quickly drew them off her hips. The man watched, an amused expression on his face.

She looked up, smiled, moistening her red lips with a delicate pointed tongue.

"You're about to be taken!" she laughed, lightly.

They stared silently at one another and then Jimmy started undressing. A few minutes later they came together in the middle of the room, their bodies pressing hard and violently at one another; their mouths cupped together, their tongues alive.

Ruth was surprised by the smoothness of the man holding her. She had expected to be the teacher, and instead found herself wonderfully

114

overwhelmed by the embrace. Excitement bolted through every nerve, leaving her weak. Finally he lifted her in his arms and moved to the bed, lying her down onto it.

Then he was on her, savagely, expertly, and hungrily. Ruth moaned as the pleasure of sensual shocks rippled through her like whip strokes. Maybe it was the build up—the awkwardness of the evening and the unexpected ability of this man. She didn't know. But suddenly Ruth realized she was in the hands of a real experienced lover; a man who knew how to make love to a girl the right way; tenderly, hungrily, savagely, excitingly.

Wave upon wave rushed oven her, churning her body in writhing convulsions. Gasping moans broke from her trembling lips. Her head thrashed from side to side, as his kisses moved over her flesh.

Then, all at once; their hips joined. Ecstasy overwhelmed her.

Ruth slumped back, exhausted, satisfied.

* * * * * * *

Carlton Turner had planned on having a steak dinner and a couple of cocktails and then return home to look over some scripts. But the first Martini blended into another and he found himself sitting in the cocktail lounge, smoking and drifting deeper and deeper into a dark, moody depression. It was a long time before he realized the cause for the depression.

Ruth.

It was the first time since she'd moved in with him that she was with another man.

The emotional effect of that thought was startling.

He finished his Martini and ordered another. When it came he looked down at it, a feeling of agonizing detachment removing his mind from the actions of his body.

Why should the idea of Ruth being with another man bother him? She was just a little tramp. Nothing more! Then his mind argued: No, that wasn't really true. She was something special; a woman with a special vitality and loveliness to her. She was hard and out-spoken; but soft and sensitive. Most people, he knew, who were outwardly hard and untouchable, were in reality soft ones inside.

Ruth had had a hard life. She had told him a lot about herself. About her life on the farm. About her father who had been loyal and loving; about her mother who had secretly had affairs with other men; about her own first sexual experience that had hardened and embittered her outlook on life; and mostly about her dreams of finding a form of respectability by getting to the top.

Yes, Carlton thought, *she was a complex of emotions and pains and hurts.*

But he had known her story—or many like it—from other women. Those others had been beautiful and they had been good bed-partners.

Yet none had affected him as much as Ruth.

Somehow his double Martini had disappeared and he ordered another. Later, another made his mind dizzy and his thoughts blurred. But one image continued to plague him: the vision of Ruth in the arms of Jimmy—the folk singer. And he didn't like it in the least.

Later, Carlton left the cocktail lounge, found his car in the parking lot and started driving down Sunset strip toward his home, but he drove past the turnoff and continued on until he had reached Highway 101, which lined the shore of the Pacific Ocean. He parked and walked out onto the sand; then sat down and watched the waves slowly making their way up the sandy beach and back into the ocean again. He stayed there for a long time, thinking; thinking about Ruth and about why he was even thinking about her at all. It was well past three in the morning when he returned to his car and drove home.

CHAPTER EIGHT

The Times column said: *"Who was out with Jimmy Belmont all might...? She was an attractive young starlet, whose name is unknown."*

Some other's read:

"Jimmy Belmont was seen last night with a young chick, known to be a new, oncoming actress. Does it mean romance?"

"What folk singer was out with what woman? And in what hotel were they were playing beddy-bye?"

"Miss Sherry Blake was seen out with Jimmy Belmont last night, doing the town. She is in an on-coming C.T film and is...so we are informed... suggested for a movie starring the famous folk singer. Is this romance, or just another of the many Hollywood 'affairs'?"

Ruth looked up from the papers, surprised. "Sherry Blake?"

"You—your new name. Didn't get around to telling you. How you like it?" Carlton inquired, taking a sip of his coffee.

"What was wrong with my own?"

He looked across the breakfast table at her, smiling. "Nothing, Ruth—just that the new one will fit your screen personality, and will look better in print.

Anyway you're stuck with it, now. Sorry I didn't warn you." Ruth bit her lower lip.

"Stop that!"

"What?"

"No lip-biting. That's a habit you'll have to stop. Remember—it doesn't do your looks any good. We can't have a star going around with chewed lips. You have to look beautiful all the time. You're a walking ad, from now on."

Ruth sighed and looked at the papers again. Most of them said the same things, hinting at what had gone on, but not coming right out and saying it in black and white. Finally she tired of them and reached for the Scotch and Soda in front of her.

"Carl."

"Yes?" He looked up at her.

"What happens next? I mean—do I have to go out with this...Jimmy? You know."

"Yes. It's good publicity. You don't know how good your show was last night. I couldn't have expected more from you." His face frowned. "I'm sorry about throwing it on you like that. But it just happened to drop in my hands—it was the best way to do it." The man was thoughtful for a moment and then said: "Strangely, I didn't like the idea of throwing you into another man's arms. A dirty business."

"Why, Carl, I *do* believe you 'like' me."

"That has nothing to do with it; and you know it, Ruth. This is a business pact. You've lived here with me because it was easier that way. Things will be changing in a couple of days."

"What does that mean?" she asked, taking another sip of her scotch.

"You're moving out. I've picked a nice, working girl's apartment for you. You'll be interviewed there. You'll be busy having publicity pictures taken. Some in the nude, for the better men's magazines."

Ruth tensed. She felt a cold sweat break out oven her body. It was the same sick reaction she'd felt about having to make the stag movie, months before. "No, Carl. Not anything dirty. I couldn't take—"

"Nothing like that. These are art pictures. They'll be nice and clean. Nothing to worry about. We can't have a star doing dirty pictures, can we?" Ruth tensed again. Sickness iced through her. For a moment she had the impulse to tell Carlton about the stag movie, and then shook it off. That might ruin things for her if he knew about it.

"No," she admitted. "It wouldn't do any good."

"Something clean and high class. Sexy—but clean sex. You can have dirty stories thrown around, but nothing like a cheap picture in a cheap magazine. Anyway—that's for next week. In the meantime, you'll have to keep in line. No drunks. No going out, unless I give you the word." He hesitated and then said: "In any case, I'll see you're kept active with Jimmy. If you want to go out—it'll either be with him or me. With me—well, we can write that one off. You're out with your promoter—manager. Purely business." Ruth studied the man's eyes, searchingly. "Is that *all* it'll be?"

Carlton laughed. "No, sweetheart. Not privately. But that's another story." He hesitated and then asked: "How *was* Jimmy?"

Ruth chewed on her lower lip, dropping her eyes. "That's a dirty question."

"So?"

"So—it's none of your damned business!" she snapped angrily, standing, taking her glass and stomping out of the room. She went to her room, slamming the door behind her.

Sitting on the bed, Ruth tried to think; tried to clear her thoughts of the confusion that had exploded there with such suddenness that it had left her dizzy.

What had made her blow the stack like that? she wondered, looking at the wall. Carl had merely asked her a question about the other man, and she'd snapped like a bitch.

She surely wasn't getting to like the man! Seriously! Especially the way she had enjoyed herself the night before with Jimmy.

Ruth considered that for a long time, puzzled. They had been together for several months, their bed shifts had been about once a week.

Ruth shook off the mental questioning and gulped her scotch. Then she lay down on the bed.

There was a knock on the door. She ignored it. The knock repeated itself.

"Go away!"

The door opened and Carlton stood there, looking at her. He didn't say anything for a long time. Then slowly he stepped forward, closing the door after him. "What's wrong?"

"Nothing, damn it!"

"Come on, Ruthie, you can't fool around with me. I know you. I've been with you for three months now, and a man gets to know something about the woman's moods and feelings. Something's wrong!" His voice was tender and soft; his face concerned.

He sat down on the bed, his hand reached for hers, lightly covering it. "Look, Ruth—you aren't getting...well, serious?"

Ruth laughed, sharply. Her eyes flashed. "God-damned, what a bastard *you* are! Serious with you? Hell and back! A woman would be crazy to get serious with you!"

Carlton frowned and then stood. "Okay. Forget it. Just that I was worried. Maybe you should take it easy tonight. Tomorrow there'll be a lot of work. Some interviews. And I want to take you out to see your apartment."

"And what am I supposed to live on?" Ruth inquired.

"That's taken care of, too. You sign a contract in the next few days. Actually it's just a legal thing—I didn't get around to it before because of our relationship. Now that things are going to change—well, it's better to make it legal. You get a few hundred a week and...when you need things, personal, I'll see you get them. The apartment is part of the deal. Okay?" He stood by the door, looking at her smiling tenderly. "You're quite a nice woman, Ruth. It's a damned shame you wanted to get into pictures."

He left.

Ruth lay there for a long time, thinking; thinking about the past months, of the nights with Carlton, and his loving hands, and his hard, skillful body, and the brutality of his instructions and directions. He was a complex man; a hard one; but a gentle, soft-hearted bastard, too.

How did she really feel about him? she wondered. It was a long time before she finally was able to stop thinking and settle down to restful sleep.

* * * * * * *

The apartment was a one bedroom affair with a small kitchen and dining room. Much like the apartment she'd lived in with John Davis; though not quite as expensive. It was just off Sunset and Vine. Carlton didn't give her more than a couple of minutes to look the place over before he hurried her out and back into the car. He drove to the *Grape Vine,* a small, intimate restaurant on Vine Street. Once inside, he led the way to a small corner booth where a short, middle-aged man was sitting, red-faced in Manhattans.

"This is Alex Hanson," Carlton introduced as they settled into the booth. "Alex, Sherry Blake."

Alex looked at Ruth and then nodded. "Alex is a press agent," Carlton explained, "and he's going to take down vital information about you—and then bend it the way he wants to, making an interesting story out of it."

Ruth laughed. "Tell the truth, and he'll have a real, spicy story," she admitted.

"Can't do that."

Alex looked up, interested. "What kind of dirt can she feed me?"

Ruth frowned, fighting back a gnawing sensation at the pit of her stomach.

"None of your business!" she snapped, nastily. She suddenly didn't like the man.

Alex laughed, but the sound was cold and harsh. His watery eyes narrowed, his thick lips drooped.

"What kind of bitch does she think she is?" he demanded of Carlton.

Ruth said "She knows what kind of woman she is—and you aren't going to stomp on me!"

Carlton laughed, nervously "Look, Alex, you know how it is with stars. They have—"

"Stars? Don't give me that, Carl. She's a *nothing* until we make her a *something*. Don't give me that. I'll do the dirty work—but she keeps her tongue shut unless spoken to. I don't have to take it from her, or anybody." The man snapped his fingers. "I could break her like that. And you with her! So just tell her who she's dealing with!"

Carlton turned his attention to Ruth. "Play ball with the man, baby. He can do you a lot of good. Please, for me?"

Ruth relaxed. "Okay. I'm sorry, Alex. We rubbed wrong. So, let's make up and be friends?"

The man glared at her for a long time, a hard look in his eyes. Then he turned to Carlton. "You hired me to push her at the public. I did a good job last night—on nothing. Okay—you pay the bills, but I don't have to like it. She goes to the top of the writing heap—but...I don't like her. Not at all. She's a tramp. I can spot them."

Ruth clawed her stomach tight. Carlton had nudged her with his knee, and she realized that it was better to remain silent.

She smiled at the man. "Look, Alex, I said I was sorry. It was a long day. Believe me—I didn't realize...I didn't know who you were. Honey, can't we be friends?" Her eyes searched the man's, a suggestion of intimacy promised in her gaze.

Alex shrugged his fat shoulders. "Call me Hanson. Mr. Hanson!"

Carlton's knee pushed Ruth's. She mentally decided to blow the ceiling off when she was alone with Carlton. *The bastard should have warmed her,* she thought. *But then he probably hadn't known that sparks would fly.*

There was a long awkward silence. Cocktails were ordered all around, but still the conversation wasn't picked up. Alex Hanson studied Ruth, during the silence, without saying a word, without showing any emotion on his face.

Finally he said, after the cocktails had been served:

"What kind of woman is she?" He was still looking at Ruth, but his question was directed to Carlton.

"A wonderful girl," Carlton announced. "You'll really like her once you get to know her."

"Yeah, I can see that!" he said without humor.

"Really, Alex—just give her a try."

"I don't have to like her to do the press-agenting for her. I don't have to give a damn about her to make the American public love the ground she walked on."

"Okay—have it your way." Carlton shrugged and gave Ruth a side-long glance, "If you weren't the best in the business—"

"Yeah, yeah, Carl." Alex laughed, oily. His eyes turned to Carlton. "Yeah, Carl, baby. I'm the best. And don't you forget it. I'll make her a star—if it's possible through publicity alone. You do the rest and we all make money. Right, baby?"

The last was directed to Ruth.

Ruth nodded and smiled warmly. The man's

eyes lowered to the dip of her dress.

"You have fun with Jimmy?" he asked.

Ruth was about to snap back a nasty remark, but Carlton's knee stopped her short.

"He's a nice boy," she offered.

"Ruth's not the kind of girl to hand out roses, Alex. She came up the hard way—and knows her business. You have to understand that she's a little hard-nosed with men—and won't let them push her too far."

"Sweet kid?" Sarcasm was thick in his voice.

"No. And she's not to be billed as a sweet kid. We want a sex angle. We want the American public to look at Sherry Blake and think sex. Every man in the country has to want to sleep with her—and think that he could, if he knew her. She's out to seduce every man in America—on the screen."

"Sounds fun," Alex admitted. "How far will she go?"

"In what way, Alex?" Carlton asked respectfully.

"Let's just say—just for begging the question—that I was interested in a little fun, on the side. How would that work out?" He didn't even look at Ruth. It was a flaunting insult; he was talking as if she wasn't even there.

"Why don't you ask her?" Carlton suggested with a surface smile. His knee jabbed Ruth's.

"I'm asking *you*." Alex pointed out coldly, his eyes boring into Carlton's.

"Nobody can speak for another person," Carlton said carefully.

"But you're different. *You* answer the question."

Ruth realized that it was a point of principle to

Alex Hanson. He wanted revenge for her insults.

"She'll do anything I tell her!" Carlton finally admitted, taking a gulp of his Martini.

Alex snapped his eyes to Ruth's. "How about it? You willing to prove he's master of this operation?"

There was no emotion, no humanity in the man's gaze. Ruth had never seen such coldness. She had always thought of herself as being pretty cold and heartless about life and about the people around her, but with Alex Hanson she had met her master. He was a first-rate son-of-a-bitch.

"Why, Mr. Hanson, somebody like you could make any woman willing. That's no test," she murmured in an innocent voice. She felt Carlton's thanks as he gently squeezed her leg under the table, out of sight of the other man.

Hanson grinned, revealing uneven teeth. His eyes gleamed. "You know, Carl, I think maybe I'll like this broad. She might be a ball to do business with, after all!" The man was silent, thinking, and then he turned toward Carlton. "I can carry on from here—without your help. Want to get to know a client, personal-like. You understand?"

"More than you know," Carlton announced, standing.

"I wasn't trying to be subtle, big man!" Alex snapped.

"I'll leave the two of you alone to get to *know* each other better," Carlton announced, as if it were all his own idea. Then without another word he turned and walked away.

Alex didn't say anything for a long time. He studied Ruth, silently, thoughtfully. Then he finally said: "You're a beautiful woman. I can see why Carl is plugging you."

"Why, *thank you*, Mr. Hanson."

"Come off the formal stuff, sweetie. Alex."

"You were the one that asked me to—"

"Forget that. It's in the past, isn't it?" The question was demanding and probing. He expected to be "yessed."

"How sweet of you." Ruth pulled tight at the nausea working at her body. It wasn't going to be pleasant letting this slob touch her.

Silence. Then.

"You don't want to stay here all day, do you, sweetie?" Ruth shrugged. "It's not a very good place to carry on the kind of interview you have in mind." The sweetness in her voice hid the subtle sarcasm that had been behind the words. The man didn't even notice.

"We can go to my place," he said, standing. As Ruth walked out of the restaurant with Hanson, she felt time had backtracked and it was a year before, and she was going to a hotel room with a slob pick up.

Not much difference, is there, Ruthie? she thought bitingly. *It all amounts to the same thing, doesn't it? They call it different names. It is done for a purpose—but it's still prostitution in a high-grade scale.*

So you've been promoted—that's all!

* * * * * * *

His apartment was nice and modern, neat. The front room had only one corner that was cluttered; that was his desk, loaded with papers, typewriter

128

and clippings from newspapers and magazines.

Alex Hanson led the way directly to the bedroom without any word of comment. Closing the door, he eyed Ruth with a cold appraising gaze.

"Strip, so I can see what's so good and mighty about you!" he snapped, nastily.

Ruth hesitated, holding down the disgust inside her.

How you've changed, she thought. *A few months of a new life and you find it insulting to be ordered around like a prostitute.*

Sighing, Ruth started undressing, finding it impossible to look the man in the eyes. This puzzled her, too. Finally she was standing before him completely naked. A cold breeze, which came into the room through an open window, chilled her flesh.

What's wrong with you, Ruth? she demanded, angry with herself. You've done this sort of thing for years. Why should it be so different, now? So awkward?

Yet she felt the humiliation of being "raped" by his pig-eyes!

She forced herself to look at the man, throwing her head back, clouding her emotions with a hardened outer shell.

That's the way, Ruth thrilled inwardly. *You're almost back to the little tramp you used to be. Think about the changes, later. But not now!*

Alex stared coldly back at her, his gaze running the full length of her body.

"Really something! You're all right. With that body—you could go far!" His voice was husky; it was the only outer sign of the effect she was having on him. "I guess you don't like me."

"Why shouldn't I like you?"

"Because of this. No woman likes to be thrown in a man's bed because he might be able to help her." His grin was cold oil.

Ruth grinned, thrusting out her hips. She moistened the surface of her lips with the point of her tongue. Her arms slid around the man's neck. It was all automatic, professional; an act she'd faked her way through so many times that she'd lost count.

Alex's smile of a man who is pleased with his power over others; his power that made women like herself bend to his wishes.

He studied her for a moment and then stepped back, and slowly removed his jacket. A little later he was embracing her against his fat naked body. Ruth mentally blocked out the man's crude love-making, trying to think of something else. Trying to fight the nausea. And the first thoughts that wedged themselves upwards to her conscious mind were:

How many more pigs would she have to sleep with?

Men like this! How long would it last? Would it be forever; or would an end come, with romance and love?

No, Ruth, you'll never have love because you're not worthy of it; you never will be loved because you're a tramp, and nobody loves a tramp!

The man was crude and brutal, moving from one breast to another, savagely nibbling, and his breath panting like a heated animal.

There had been many men like this in Ruth's prostitute days, but for some reason, which she couldn't understand, this disgusted her, now. Fluttering sensation wiggled through her nerves, tickled

130

the lining of her stomach.

Won't he ever stop? she wondered, trying to hurry the man along with her hands.

All her life, selling her body, like this, and now it disgusted her. Why? Ruth wondered, annoyed by the questions.

Don't think about it. Think about something else.

This man will help you. He'll help to make you a public image.

But is it worth it?

Damn it all, Ruth, of course it's worth it! The very fact that you're disgusted shows that it's more than worth it. A subtle change has come over you in the past months; and that change is for the good.

The man pressed down to her; she knew it was almost over. A sigh of relief shuddered over her.

* * * * * * *

The cocktail lounge was dark; intimate.

Ruth was drunk. It was like swimming through thick fog, and in a vague way she was happy. As happy as it was possible to be.

It had been necessary to go out and get smashed, after Alex Hanson. The taste of him was still in her.

It was strange how many changes had taken place since her arrival to Los Angeles. It was almost as if she were another person.

More drinks filled her stomach, and she realized it wouldn't be long before she buzzed out of the picture. Paying for the last drink, Ruth walked out into the night world. It wasn't far to the apartment Carlton had rented for her.

A little later she was lying on the bed, in the small bedroom, smoking and trying to relax the tension of her mind.

Where, now, little girl? To stardom? Or... where? Ruth realized that it would take time to answer that last question. She only hoped it wouldn't be too long. Maybe, once she'd made it to the top, it wouldn't be so hand for her—maybe then it would be possible to stay away from men who didn't matter. Maybe she would find love.

Ruth tensed against that last realization.

Was there a man that really mattered to her?

The form of Carlton Turner focused before her mind's eye.

Yes, there was a man that mattered, but he was the kind that wouldn't hook to a tramp like herself. He was too high—too far above her—he knew too much about her.

No, Ruth, you'll have to forget that idea. Carlton Turner doesn't have time for you in a personal way—he'll promote you to stardom, and he'll make love to your body, when it pleases him to do so, but that's all—nothing more!

A sigh broke from her lips and she settled back, closing her eyes, blotting out all thought, all confusion, and all the loneliness that had suddenly wedged itself through her.

Sleep came fast.

CHAPTER NINE

The next morning, when Ruth went to Carlton's home, she was greeted at the door by Alex Hanson and a couple of photographers.

"Where you been ?" the man asked, acidly.

"Where's Carl?"

"In his study. He's been wondering where you were."

Ruth stepped around Hanson and into the large, bookcase lined study. Carlton Turner looked up, frowning.

"I was at the apartment," she explained before he could say anything.

Carlton slapped his forehead and then groaned "I should have thought of that. Why didn't you?— oh, never mind! There's a lot of work to be done. I've lined up some magazine publicity. Alex wants some pictures of you—around the town. After that you report to the studio for a screen test with Jimmy Belmont. The movie is going through much faster than we thought it would. I've been pushing for some backing for the movie in which you are starring with Jimmy—and the little stunt you did with him the other day cinched the deal. You're in for a real wild time from now on. I'll have somebody move your stuff to the apartment, today. You drive, don't you?"

Ruth frowned and nodded. "Why?"

"I'll have a studio car assigned to you. I can't be driving you all over the place. You'll be on your own from now on. And—we'll have a phone in your apartment by tomorrow. Another thing," he stepped up to her placing an arm around her shoulder, "there's a contract to sign. When you're at the studio this afternoon report to my office."

"Think you have enough for me to do in one day?" she laughed excitedly.

"Enough for today. I'll give you a copy of the script this afternoon. Take a look at it tonight. Tomorrow you and Jimmy do the town again."

"Again?" She felt disappointed. All of a sudden a huge pit had formed between them and she felt lost and alone.

"Again—and again. There's talk around town— so we'll keep it alive."

They were starting out of the office. Ruth stopped, turned to face Carl and said, "Carl— what—what about us?"

He frowned, started to say something, changed his mind and kissed her forehead. "We'll be seeing each other. Don't worry."

They walked into the living room. Alex was talking to the photographers, but stopped the moment he saw them. He turned toward Carlton.

"Can we get things started, now?" he demanded.

"Alex, Alex, boy—you'll never live to be a hundred and one at your pace," Carlton soothed.

"Who wants to be a hundred and one? I'll settle for sixty."

"And be lucky getting there."

134

"Yeah, with guys like you around to drive me out of my mind." His eyes flashed to Ruth. "Is that what she's going to wear?"

"No. You guys have some drinks while I show Ruth her new clothes." Carlton led the way across the room to the hallway that went to the small bed-room where Ruth had been living the last few months.

"What's this about clothes?" Ruth inquired.

"A new star has to have a little of everything." Carlton squeezed her arm. "And, anyway, I wanted to buy you a few things."

"I don't understand you, Carl," Ruth announced, as they stepped into the bedroom. "I don't get you at all."

"How's that?"

"Well...the way you treat me. Why? Maybe I'm still an innocent, but I thought we were...damn it all! I guess we weren't really lovers!"

Carlton laughed harshly, closing the door. "Look, Sweetheart, I told you we'd make you a star—and that's what we're doing. Nothing can get in the way of that. We agreed on this right from the beginning." The man hesitated for a moment and then said: "Okay, I'll admit you were getting to me. I can't afford emotional ties now. So...this is the easiest way to make things simple for me. Before things get too sticky—we break it off."

Ruth felt a chill; she wanted to cry, but didn't know why.

"You're the damndest man I've ever known!" Emotion choked her voice. With effort she fought back tears.

Carlton reached for her and pulled her closer to

him. His lips caressed her cheek and then sought out her mouth. They kissed, tenderly, and then passionately.

After a while, he pulled away. "Ruth—this is best—for both of us. Believe me. It could have been done differently but this is probably the best way. Neither of us can afford complications, now. You'd be surprised how much interest you caused with that Jimmy Belmont thing. Not that people care about *you*—but with Alex doing the press-agenting, everybody in town is listening to what he says."

"That's another thing, Carl. That was a dirty trick you pulled!" she snapped, glaring at him. "You could have warned me about Alex!"

"Sorry. I didn't think it would go like that. The man's a bastard—but knows his business. We need him." Carlton hesitated. He clenched his hands into tight fists and turned away. "Look in the closet—you'll find a few things you'll want there." He walked to the door and left, without another word.

Ruth stared at the closed door, stunned, shaking. *What could have caused him to do that?* she wondered.

Damn men! And double-damn Carlton Turner, she cursed, savagely.

* * * * * * *

Carlton Turner walked hurriedly through the living room, ignoring the men, and then into his den, slamming the door after him. For a few minutes he stood there, leaning against the wall, weak.

"Why're you shaking, Carl?" he said softly, clamping hands against his face. He stood there for a long time, thinking about Ruth. She had become an important part of his life. He hadn't realized that until the other day, when he had to throw her into the arms of Jimmy Belmont. The idea of Ruth's body in the arms of another man caused nagging needles of guilt to stab his mind and twist his guts.

"She's getting to you, Carl. Forget her. She's on her way up, and there's nothing you can do about it. Ruth's the type of woman that would spit in your face if you lowered the romantic crap on her. She wants to make the big time, and if you don't ride along with her, she'll find somebody else who will. It's too late. People know she's alive, now."

Slowly he relaxed and then moved across the room to his large desk. He tried to put Ruth out of his mind and think about the business at hand that needed his immediate attention. It was a long time before he could center his attention on the pile of papers on the desk before him.

* * * * * * *

The day was hectic for Ruth. First the pictures. Some in Hollywood, and a few in Santa Monica. They had to break for lunch, and then Alex drove her to the studio where she went to Carlton's office.

Carlton was business, and impersonal, almost insulting in his attitude to her.

"Sign here," he demanded, when the contracts were brought into his office by his secretary.

* * * * * * *

"What's it say?" Ruth countered, staring at him.

137

"Standard six-year contract at two-fifty a week, with salary boosts at the proper times. Just sign and—I'll have somebody take you to the dressing room for the test with Jimmy. We need something to show the backers. Probably be shooting till late tonight."

"Signing my life away?" Ruth questioned, studying the man carefully. For a moment longer she hesitated, and then decided it didn't make that much difference.

The man was giving her her big chance. If she was going to trust him with her career, she would trust him with the legal matters.

Fifteen minutes later she was in a dressing room.

Make-up men did over her face and put a red wig on her head. When they were finished, she looked like a teenage sex-bomb.

They rushed Ruth to the small set on Stage 1, which was a small bachelor apartment living room. Lighting men had already done their work; the camera crew was lining up shots and the director was shouting instructions to Jimmy who was standing in front of the camera.

Ruth was handed a script by a young assistant director. The pages were marked, to cover the scene. It was a love scene. She and Jimmy were supposed to be on the couch, making love to her. There were just a half a dozen spoken lines, the rest was sensual action.

Ruth grinned to herself and settled in the chair that had been given her. She waited until called, reading through the scene over and over again until she believed it was fixed in her mind forever.

138

Mr. Niles, the director, finally came over to her and said: "You understand the scene, honey?"

Ruth nodded.

"You see, baby, it's this way. You are in love with Jimmy—you're star struck, you want to sleep with him—but, of course we can't have anything like that going on. There'll be a cut at the most dramatic moment, and everything is left to the imagination. I want you to understand that. We can't be too sexy here. But—you'll play it up big. You want sex; you want Jimmy to love you and to marry you. This is the big scene in the film. The teenagers should be breathless. But we can't have them being demoralized. Make it sexy, but with a breathless, childish attitude. Dreamland. Fantasy for all those kids out there watching. Make them want you. In their dreams or sexual fantasies. Understand?"

"Any time you're ready," Ruth announced, ignoring the question.

The man stared at her and then grinned. "Fine, baby. We can start, now."

He motioned Ruth to the set.

Ruth sat on the couch, next to Jimmy. The cameraman lined up the shot and the director went through the scene with them. The lights were adjusted, and about twenty minutes after she'd settled down beside the singer, the director suggested a run through.

On cue, Ruth turned and faced Jimmy, placing her arms around him.

"Oh, Danny, don't you understand how I feel about you?" she whispered in a high, innocent voice.

Jimmy caressed her hair and smiled. "You know

how I am," he said softly.

Ruth's hand moved up to his neck, drawing him to her. Their lips met, lingered and then she pulled away, fire in her eyes. "Is that all you can do? Don't you know how to kiss a woman?"

"You're just a girl," he scolded, grinning.

"More of a woman than *you* know," she smiled, suggestively.

Jimmy looked at the bedroom—on, rather where the bedroom was supposed to be. "*That* much of a woman?"

She tensed, pushed away from him and then turned, unsure of herself. "I want you, Jimmy—but I want you the way every decent girl wants her man."

"Cut!" shouted the director, and then remembering it was a trial run, he stepped up to Ruth. "His name is *not* Jimmy!"

"I'm sorry, Mr. Niles. I just got all worked up—forgot."

"Okay, try it again. After you said 'but I want you the way every decent girl wants her man,' you embrace, happily. He'll draw you into his arms and you'll kiss. That's the end of the scene. Just hold it there and I'll indicate when to relax. Okay, baby?"

They went through it again. Then a couple of times more. After that they tried a first take. Then another. Then another. After that it was for close ups. It was well after seven when everything was wrapped up and the director said they could go home.

Jimmy caught her at the stage door.

"How about a date?" he offered.

Ruth looked at him, remembering what Carlton had told her. She considered.

140

"Finish the scene the way it should be finished," Jimmy explained. "You really were hot! I mean...so sexy!"

She shrugged. "Why shouldn't we? That's what we're supposed to be doing, anyway; so we might as well have the fun!"

* * * * * * *

Jimmy left late in the morning. He had made love to her when they awoke. He kissed her at the door when he left.

Ruth sat in the front room, gazing out into the blankness of space. *Jimmy was good at the bed-routine,* she thought, vaguely annoyed by the fact. But it had meant nothing to her.

"What's wrong with you? You're fussing, oven nothing!"

Just then there was a knock on the door and she got up, and answered it.

Carlton Turner was standing there, a haggard expression on his face.

"Can I come in?" he asked, awkwardly. His voice was tired and there were dark circles under his eyes.

"Sure." Ruth stepped back. The man closed the door and then strode across the room. He turned and looked at her.

"Ruth—I—" Carlton hesitated, lowered his eyes and then cursed under his breath.

"What's wrong?" she inquired, surprised by his attitude; by his very presence; by his appearance.

"I had to see you." Carlton collapsed on the sofa, staring up at her. "You got me unnerved—but

141

good."

"What?" She couldn't believe what he was saying. It didn't seem possible.

"Okay—so it's stupid. But...hell! I can't help it. I've known a lot of women—but none that hit me like you have. Something about you—don't ask me what! Anyway—I was up all night...thinking... damned thinking!" Carlton rubbed his face with his hands and then continued: "I feel like a foolish teenager. Dumb! Really dumb! And I don't like this whole thing."

Ruth started to say something and then stopped herself. *Wait,* her mind warned, *until you've let him hang himself!*

"Look—can't we...oh, hell!"

Carlton stood and moved up to Ruth. Without warning he crushed her to him. His lips touched hers.

After a few moments the man lifted Ruth into his arms and carried her into the bedroom, laying her down on the bed.

"This is what I want!" he almost cursed, moving down to her, starting to pull aside her blouse. In minutes he had stripped her naked and his hands started playing over her body with savage hunger and passionate need. Ruth had never seen him this way, and it was impossible to do anything but lie there, letting him have her, without a struggle. His caresses fired oven her body, searching, touching her breasts, running across her stomach, down over her thighs, whispering like soft electric fingers, charging the nerves and cells of her flesh. Fevered excitement rushed over Ruth, and a soft moan escaped from her parted lips.

142

She didn't have time to completely understand what was happening. She wasn't given a moment to think about the strangeness of this new event. The man had somehow undressed, while caressing her, and then moved down, driving his body hard against hers. After that, she didn't think about anything.

* * * * * * *

After having made love to Ruth, Carlton Turner stood up, got dressed and hurried out of her apartment. He walked for a long time, still puzzled by what had happened. When he'd first gone to her apartment there hadn't been any mental awareness as to what he planned to do. The restless night had plagued him, had numbed his thinking; had dulled his sense of timing. That morning he'd gotten up, had several drinks and then drove to Ruth's apartment.

What's wrong with you, bastard? he mentally questioned, stepping into a bar.

He ordered a double Martini and waited.

Ruth's just a slut. A bitch. A hot chick. A woman who wants to climb her way up into stardom. And that's all you are for her—a way to get there. And you shouldn't think of her in any other way.

The drink came. He downed it and ordered another. He was drinking too much; but didn't care at that moment. He knew that Ruth was something special. Something that was more than just a good lay or a little tramp. She'd come up the hard way, and had used her body to get ahead. It was all she'd learned in life. He couldn't blame her for doing that. Some would call her a tramp. Some might say she

143

was nothing but a free spirit, finding a way through life using the tools nature had been so generous in handing out to her.

He slowly sipped the second cocktail, and when it was finished, paid for the drinks and left.

He drove to his office and told his secretary not to bother him. He sat at his desk for a long time, thinking about Ruth, and about what he was doing to her. It was a dirty business; and he couldn't stop what was being done. To cut off the affair between Jimmy and Ruth, now, would be to end her chances for the movie he'd picked out for her. There were other movies—but too much money had been directly invested in Ruth to back down.

Damned women! And damn his luck to have met this woman who had a sexual attractiveness that drove men out of their minds with desire. Damn her body and her willingness to please, and damn her wonderful love making.

Finally the necessities of the business-day overpowered his thoughts of Ruth, and even though they kept creeping up in his mind, he managed to take care of his work. It wasn't until later that he thought of her again in agonizing frustrations. He was alone in his house, sipping Scotch, when intimate, sensual thoughts of Ruth aggravated him in full force. He tried to get her by phone, but the operator didn't have any new listing under her name.

Cursing, Carlton returned to the home bar and mixed himself another drink. He was creating a monster in his own life—and was too late to do anything about it.

PART IV

CHAPTER TEN

During the days that followed, Ruth had little time to think seriously about Carlton Turner. Most of the daylight hours were spent with Alex, dress designers, directors, and dramatic coaches. The rest of her time was filled with and studying her part in the up-coming movie. The nights were crowded with dining out, going to panties and being seen with Jimmy Belmont. She saw little of Carlton, but when she was in the quiet of her bedroom, she would find her thoughts drifting back to the morning when he had come to her. Only a fool would have thought that Carlton wasn't starting to get serious. Ruth wasn't a fool. She knew Carlton too well not to realize the change in the man's attitude. When they accidentally happened upon one another at the studio, he was distant and impersonal. Another giveaway sign concerning his feeling towards her.

Jimmy became a strangely important part of Ruth's life. She didn't love him. That would be impossible for her to do. Jimmy wasn't the kind of man that could hold a woman like her. Nevertheless, she found pleasure in his company and enjoyable excitement in his arms.

The nights were long, sensual sprees when

Jimmy shared Ruth's bed. They were lonely and restless when she was alone. At such time she found herself thinking about Carlton Turner. A couple of times she almost phoned him to ask the man over. She thought of the wonderful joy when held in his arms. She wanted him there to make love to her.

The days drifted and melted together, becoming a blur of hard work during the days and hot sex in the evenings. Two weeks ran together into a Mardi gras of activity; but a continued loneliness welled over Ruth. It was Friday night. Ruth was alone in her apartment. Monday morning was to be the first shooting day of the Belmont movie. It would be her first day as a star and she was high. She was thinking about Carlton; about how much she missed him; how much she wanted him to be with her.

It was about one in the morning when the front door bell rang. Without moving from the chair in which she'd been sitting, Ruth asked who it was.

"It's Carl. Let me in!"

Her pulse raced. Excitement rushed through her. She staggered across the room, opened the door and then closed it behind Carlton Turner.

He merely glared at her, saying nothing. A strange expression was on his face. His eyes were narrowed, as if he were attempting to hide the thoughts that might reveal themselves there.

"You've been drinking, haven't you?" Ruth accused, trying to conceal the emotion in her voice.

"I had to see you," Carlton announced, finally coming out of his daze. He walked to the sofa, sat down and lit a cigarette without looking at her.

"Why?" She looked at the man and felt a sudden inner thrill.

148

He's a mark, signed, sealed and delivered; helpless! she thought. But the idea didn't give her the satisfaction that it might have many months before; it merely excited her emotions.

"I...don't know what's coming over me, Ruth...but I don't like you living here. I've thought about it for days, now. Every night I think about you. It doesn't make sense. But...I want you back. No other woman has...they bore me! I've tried...but all I remember is you."

For a moment she almost believed he was about to say he loved her.

"You're a wonder in bed," he stated, almost unemotional, almost distant. "I've known a lot of broads, but you're the best."

She remained silent, uncertain what he was trying to say. The confusion of her own thoughts and reactions held her back from daring to suggest she felt he was so terribly special. In fact, that very idea was frightening to her.

"We'll kill this thing between you and Jimmy as soon as the movie is released. It won't be too hard. And you can just be seen in public and then return to me...without any over night stops with him. We'll keep the papers happy but you won't be going out alone with him any more than necessary!"

Ruth stared at him, amazed. His face was drawn and tired. Now that he'd let his barriers down, his eyes revealed the struggle he was going through.

"What are you really saying, Carl?" she demanded, just a little blandly, afraid to reveal her own feelings.

"That I want you there...within easy reach. Just like before. I want things back like they were! Is that difficult to understand?"

He wanted an easy, live-in hot lay! That was what he was telling her, indirectly, glossed over; but stripped down to the bare bones that's what he wanted. This hurt on a level that was unnerving. Yet what else could a woman like herself really expect?

Love? Well, that was romantic idealism. Her chances of that kind of thing were dim at best. She choked down the sense of pain. The facts were basic; she was on the verge of a career as an actress, and that would change things in her life; many desirable men would be around to chase after her. She could have her pick. Love? Hardly. But Ruth had been used all her life; and only in the last years had she learned how to use back.

Instinct, rather than emotion, caused her to say:

"What if I don't like that deck of cards? What if I like being here...?" She regretted it right away; but couldn't take it back.

Carlton squinted at Ruth and then a low, animal sound broke from his lips. "You do as I say, Miss! You do *exactly* as I tell you! You're mine, body and soul—and don't you forget it!"

"You really mean it, don't you?" Fear mixed with tenderness; and the result was an edge of anger. What right did this man have to push her around; order her as if she were an animal? Then the anger softened as she realized how much Carlton had actually given her; how much he'd done for her. Even though his methods were sometimes brutal and cruel—they had been effective. She was on her way to the top where nobody would be able to really touch her.

"I mean it, Ruth. I didn't realize how important

you were until after you were here—out of my home and out of my personal life. I was afraid of you; afraid of what you might mean to me if I saw too much of you."

Ruth studied him, seriously, almost grimly, uncertain how to respond.

"I didn't think you were the kind of man who could really care about a woman. You were too busy—to get involved—I believe you told me that, one time." Her voice was cold; but inside she was suppressing torrid emotions. She was thinking about all those nights when she wanted to be with Carlton.

"I don't know. I just don't know. What is being serious—anyway?" Carlton stood and moved closer to Ruth. "I'm serious in the way I want you—but I can't say it's anything emotional. Maybe it's merely physical—I don't know. But I want you back. Things were pretty nice when you were around...pretty nice."

His arms went around her waist, drawing her closer to him. She felt the familiar thrill at his nearness; of his words.

Could a man really care enough for her to marry her? No! He wanted her as a mistress. He wanted her to be around the house to play with when he was in the mood. He wanted her body; not herself!

Then his lips covered hers and she stopped thinking for a long time. She was only aware of the thrill of their bodies closely locked in the tight, hungry embrace. Nothing else mattered.

Then he pulled away.

"Please, Ruth. Come back to the house. It'll be easier that way—I can help you on the script each night—give you pointers, so you won't screw things us…I mean…after all, you're a new, totally inexperienced actress and even if your instincts are great, this is serious business…and—"

"That's it—isn't it?" Ruth snapped, hurt. He wanted to make sure that she managed to run through the scenes each day, so that the film ran through quickly and smoothly. "You're afraid I'll blow it for you…"

"No, Ruth—that isn't that, it's you. Believe me." But Ruth wasn't listening anymore. The emotions that had moved over her in the last minutes now drained away. All that was left was a cold resignation. Even if he was some what taken by her skill as a sexual object, even if he might have some kind of momentary fascination, the bottom line was he had invested a lot of money and energy in her; and that, literally, was very important to the man. He wasn't offering love; he was offering a continuation of a business deal that included sexual favors. To him she was a cheap lay. He understood her days as a prostitute; and that spoiled everything. No man would love her; no man would care anything about her; because she was a tramp and would never be anything else to any man.

"If that's what you want, Carl…maybe it'll be better for the picture." She turned away from him and thought: *more fun for you—more fun using my body; getting your money's worth.*

"I don't know about you, Carl, but I'm going to bed. You have somebody come over tomorrow to help me with my things." She started for the bedroom. "Help yourself to the booze—if that's what you want—I'm tired." As she stepped into the bedroom she called over her shoulder: "I need my beauty rest for tomorrow's shot. Goodnight!"

There was a sharp intake of breath from Carlton, and then silence. After a long time, Ruth heard the front door open and slam shut. Silence followed. She lay there for a long time, fighting the urge to cry. She kept telling herself that no man was worth being emotional about; that Carlton Turner was a no-good slob, not worth crying over. But the tears finally won out, and she lay across the bed, clawing at her face, trying to hold back the moisture with her fingers.

It was a long time before exhaustion finally overwhelmed her sobbing and she fell into a restless sleep.

* * * * * * *

The next day Ruth moved back into Carlton Turner's home. She had expected him to approach her, make love to her. That night he threw a large party at which Jimmy Belmont was her escort. Photos were taken of the two of them kissing, drinking, dancing together. Carlton didn't say more than a few words to Ruth; and then only to give her and Jimmy instructions on what they were to do for the publicity cameras. It was late when the party finally broke up. She only saw Carlton long enough to say good-night.

He didn't even kiss her then.

Jimmy had made no attempt to make a pass at her, and Ruth guessed that he'd been given instructions to lay off.

Alone in her room, Ruth thought about Carlton, somewhere in the large house, by himself. It was some time before sleep came.

The next morning Carlton wasn't up until eleven. They sat at the breakfast table without saying anything. She could tell that the man was in one of his distant moods. He gazed off into space, and sat there for a long time without moving. When coffee was served he finally turned his attention toward Ruth.

"How'd you like the party?" he asked. His eyes moved over her body, as if he was able to see through the robe to the nudity of her flesh. She felt a hot rush. She lowered her gaze and looked into the blackness of her coffee. She didn't answer for a few moments.

"Carl," she finally said, "what's with you?"

The man looked away. "What do you mean?"

"You haven't tried anything...with me," she accused in a biting voice.

"What did you expect?" He was still looking away from her, across the room at the blank wall.

"Well...after the other night I—I half expected to be...raped!" She laughed at that. "Well?"

He retorted with: "Ruth, I said I had to have you around—and I meant that I couldn't stand the idea of you being in the arms of another man—but I didn't say that we were going to rush right into a hot affair. I want to think things out. You puzzle me." For the first time since they had started talking, he looked at her. "You're a deeply puzzling woman—"

"I don't see why you say that."

"But you are. You're beautiful—but more than that. Maybe I've not been as close to a woman as I—no—that's not quite true, either. Hell! I don't want to think about it."

154

Ruth found herself fighting a sense of satisfaction and pain. The old Ruth saw simply a mark, helpless in her control. The new Ruth saw a man who was very powerful, and certainly *not* in her control.

They finished their coffee without talking. Afterwards he suggested they go through the scene the director was going to shoot the next morning.

It was late in the afternoon when they finished and Ruth went to her room, undressed and had a shower. She was just stepping out of the bathroom when there was a knock on the door.

"Yes?"

The door opened and Carlton stepped in. He was dressed in a silk bathrobe. His eyes rushed over the nakedness of her body, desire slowly starting to burn there.

"What you want?" she demanded, startled by his sudden entrance.

Without a word Carlton stepped up to Ruth. His arms went around her body, hungrily drawing her against him. Their lips met, open and moist, their tongues lashed out at one another.

Ruth felt suddenly weak. Emotion ripped through her. All at once she had the wild idea that she was in love.

It was like being home at last, as if for the first time in her life she had found a place that was her own. They didn't speak as he lifted her into his arms and carried her to the bed. She lay down, waiting while the man pulled aside his robe and moved down to the bed, next to her.

His hands stroked oven her breasts and then along the flat of her stomach.

"Oh, Ruth—I'd almost forgotten how wonderful your body is," he murmured.

A tremor writhed over her. Emotion slowly choked a tight knot in her throat and suddenly she was sobbing and not knowing why. Insane happiness caused murmuring laughter to break from her trembling lips.

Oh, how good it was to be with Carl! she thought. *Good! God, how good!*

If only she could love him; if only he could love her. She would be happy for the rest of her life with a man like Carl.

The realization of the implications of that thought froze Ruth. For a moment she forgot the pleasure of the man; she forgot the stabbing rhythm of the weight on her hips. Then a choking gasp exploded from her lips as ecstasy broke away all thoughts, making her aware of the man and the love and the pleasure all at once.

She lay there for a long time without moving. Carlton was beside her, relaxed in the half-sleep aftermath of sex.

When she did move, Carlton sat up, reaching for her. She turned, facing him and realized that tears were running down her cheeks.

"Ruth," Carlton said in a husky voice, "I love you. I know that. I realized it when I saw your naked body. I've been fighting it for days; fighting with every nerve." Ruth shook her head from side to side. "No, Carl. You don't love me. You couldn't love me."

She thought about all the dirty things she'd done in the past; and about the dirtiest: the stag film she'd made during her first week in Los Angeles. *No, no*

156

man should love a tramp like herself.

"I love you, Ruth. I don't know how long. I know that I need you right now. I can't explain it—but...*hell!*" He buried his lips against hers.

Ruth drew her body closer to his and they strained together.

He did love her, in his way. And for the moment it should be enough for her. How long will it last? she wondered. *How long would their love last?*

And suddenly she realized, without any doubt, that she loved Carlton Turner, too. And with that realization a terrible depression overwhelmed her

It was one thing for a man like Carlton to love a woman like herself—for a while—but another thing when the woman loved the man, in return. She was a professional, detached. She should remain so. She couldn't with him.

Ruth knew that her love was something more lasting than she would have thought possible. She was sure that Carlton would never feel the same way.

As their bodies surged together for the second time, Ruth's mind formed the words that had plagued her for years, now:

Nobody loves a tramp!

Then she added: *at least, not for very long!*

After that all thoughts blurred in the pleasure of the man. Ecstasy burst. Awareness blackened. Exhaustion covered her mind and body. She wasn't even aware of falling asleep.

CHAPTER ELEVEN

Ruth went through the first days of shooting in a confused emotional daze. She was both excited by Carlton's sudden declaration of love and the thrill of making her first, *real* picture.

Everybody was calling her "Baby," "Darling," "Sweetheart," in the usual Hollywood tradition; but it only meant something when Carlton Turner used those words. In private he was love and romance; in public he was distant and cool; all business. But that was part of the game they had to play out; a part that chilled Ruth every time she thought of it.

Nobody loves a tramp! she kept telling her emotions so that when Carlton had tired of her it wouldn't be too emotional a thing.

At night, in Carlton's arms, Ruth discovered the warmth and extent of his love. It was almost possible to really believe that he could actually love her in the way a man was meant to love a woman. Cradled in his arms, after their love-making, she was completely convinced their love was a perfection that would never end.

But it was away from Carlton, and the spell his nearness created, that Ruth was forced to face reality; and depression would settle. Then, on the last day of shooting, early in the morning, Ruth received

158

a note that had been handed the gate guard.

Sitting in her dressing room, she tore it open, wondering from who it might be.

The letter was neatly typed, and its contents were cruelly pointed.

> *"Dear Miss Browne:*
>
> *"If you don't want Carlton Turner to find out about your first movie, meet me at the address listed below at nine this evening.*
>
> *"Allen Anson."*

Panic caused a sick nausea to rush over Ruth. For a long time she sat there in the dressing room, dizziness swimming around her head. It was the maid, who stepped up to her, and said the director was waiting, which snapped her momentarily out of the daze.

Standing, Ruth started for the set just outside her dressing room.

"Hi there, baby," Hank Niles greeted, patting her shoulder. "Get your beauty sleep last night?" Ruth didn't say anything. She moved into the small office set and turned toward the camera.

Somebody said something to her, but she didn't hear. Her mouth was dry and her lips trembled.

Niles, the director, stepped up to her, said "What's wrong, baby?"

"Nothing," Ruth managed, shaking her head. The next minutes blurred. Somebody was shouting at her. She didn't hear them.

Her mind kept racing over the words of the letter. She kept mentally picturing what it would be like if Carlton Turner found out about the stag movie she'd made. It could ruin his picture; it could ruin her career.

All she could think about was what Anson would be wanting from her.

She knew it would be some kind of blackmail; but what?

Somehow the hours managed to slip by; she never remembered doing anything. All her actions and all her words were motions she managed to go through. When they were finished late in the afternoon, Ruth rushed to her dressing room, put on a coat and left the set. She found a phone booth outside the studio stage, and dialed John Davis' number.

Maybe he could help her.

After the tenth ring, she hung up, stepped from the phone booth and started off the lot.

Twenty minutes later she was sitting in a cocktail lounge, drinking a Martini.

A lot had happened to her since the day she'd been forced into making that dirty film for Allen Anson. She'd come a long way.

Now it seemed everything was circling back; her past was returning to shatter everything that had happened.

After her third Martini, Ruth went to the phone booth in the lounge and dialed John's number again. He was the only man who might be able to help her; the only person alive with whom she could talk to, honestly, unafraid.

On the third ring the phone was picked up on

the other end.

"Hello?" John's voice came over the receiver.

Ruth felt a sense of complete relief. John would think of something to help her.

"This is Ruth," she announced in an emotionally choked voice.

For a moment only silence answered her and then a gasp sounded in the receiver.

"Ruth—how nice to hear from you. What's new?" he asked.

Ruth hesitated and then swallowed hard, said: "John, you said that if I ever needed a friend that—"

"What is it? What happened?" His voice sounded alarmed; honestly concerned and interested. Ruth thrilled. John was the first man who had ever meant anything other than a quick tumble and a twenty dollar bill. Her first male friend.

"Can you meet me here? I have—something terrible came up. I need you—" Her voice cracked and suddenly she realized it wouldn't be possible to continue for a moment.

Maybe nobody loved a tramp—but she knew one man who liked one enough to help her.

"Where are you?"

Ruth managed to give the address of the lounge and John hurriedly said he'd be there in half an hour. She hung up the phone and stood there for a long time, fighting for emotional control.

Finally she opened the door and stepped into the cocktail lounge. This time she found a corner booth that was darkened and more private than any other spot in the room.

She waited.

* * * * * * *

It took Ruth about ten minutes to bring John up to date and tell him about the letter she'd received from Allen Anson. She had watched his face as she'd spoken, trying to feel the thoughts behind his expressions. He had remained completely blank; revealing nothing.

"That bastard!" was John's first reaction when she had finished her story.

"What can I do?" Ruth pleaded, reaching for the man's hand and squeezing it between her hands.

"Go see him. First. Second—we'll have to play it from there." He looked into her eyes and then said: "I'm glad you felt you could turn to me for help."

"Oh, John, you don't know what a day I went through! I felt as if the world had collapsed. I couldn't tell Carlton—and...I didn't know who to turn to. I had to talk to somebody; somebody who would understand, and want to help. I didn't know for sure if you would be willing to..."

John lowered his eyes and said: "I'd do anything for you, Ruth. I didn't realize until too late that I really loved you. Well, in my foolish way!"

She wanted to say something to that but found the words were lost, choked up in emotional anguish.

"Anyway, Ruthie, I know that's gone and past—but you're the kind of woman that cries so much for love, needs it so much, that a man can't help loving you. Some women are like that—no matter what they are. A woman needs only to be wanted, to be protected, to be loved, to have all those things.

162

That's the way life is. A man will forgive a woman anything, if he loves her; and he'll love her if she's the kind that hungers so much for it—like you do. You've changed a lot since we saw each other last."

Words came, then: "I've changed...but I'm afraid not enough." Then she suddenly told him of her doubts about the true feelings of Carlton for her; and she revealed her own feelings for the man.

"Maybe he *does* love you—Ruth. You're not hard to love."

"Maybe, for you—but he's not the kind of man that needs my type of woman. Anyway—nobody loves a tramp!"

"I do—and you aren't a tramp!"

"A nice lie—thanks." Ruth squeezed his hands affectionately.

"Let's get the hell out of here and surprise dear little old Anson!" John snapped angrily.

* * * * * * *

They had knocked at Anson's apartment door a couple of minutes before they got an answer.

The door opened and the fat, little man stood there, looking sleepily out. For a moment his face revealed no emotion and then he grinned and stepped back. "Come on in. I didn't expect you so early—or with your little friend, Ruthie. I was catching a little rest and—"

"Shut up!" John Davis snapped angrily, slamming the door behind him and pressing close to the man.

"Simmer down, Davis. Don't be a fool—you know better than to push me around—I'll just warn

163

you once!" Anson's face was hard. His eyes narrowed.

John stepped away from the other man and said: "What's the deal? What kind of dirty deal did you have in mind?"

Anson took his time answering. Then he merely said: "That's what I invited this young lady here to talk about. Would you two like a drink?"

"No—and neither do you! " John pointed out in a hard voice.

Anson started to move and then froze in his tracks. He turned his eyes to Ruth and grinned. "You think this little playboy is going to be of some help to you? He wouldn't dare touch me! You both know that!"

Ruth felt a sickening grind whip through her stomach and then up her spine. It was true. It had been the threat of violence from Anson that had caused her to make the film for him.

"Now, my little fellows," Anson slowly continued, starting across the room toward a small table on which was a bottle of whiskey, "let's talk!"

He was quiet as he poured himself a drink and downed part of it.

He turned. Faced Ruth. "I want fifty percent of your earnings for my silence. Plus a...couple of thousand up front to pay for the expenses of making the film. I'll give you all the negatives and the prints once you have signed a personal contract with me cutting me in on half of everything. After all, I helped to discover you—I gave you your first break!"

John was already half across the room. He reached for the man and a fist smashed into the fat stomach.

Anson doubled over, the air burst from his white lips. His eyes bugged and a gasping sound came from his throat.

Davis slapped him a couple of times across the face with the back of his fist.

Finally John Davis said: "How did that feel, little man?"

"I'll have you killed, Johnny-boy. I'll have you killed!" Anson announced.

The look in the little man's eyes tore terror through Ruth. She knew the threat was a promise. Cold ice rippled over her and suddenly she was numb, feeling nothing. There was nothing she could do but make the deal with Anson; if for no other reason than to save John Davis' life.

"You can have your contract—but don't touch John!" she announced. "That's the condition! Take it or leave it!"

The two men turned, looked at her. Davis was white faced with surprise, Anson was grinning crookedly.

"Plus another couple of thousand—because of the little job your friend here has done to me," Anson hissed between broken and bleeding lips.

Ruth nodded. "When do you want the four Gs?" She didn't know how she'd get it; but somehow she would have to.

Ruth felt suddenly sick and weak. It was only with extreme effort that she kept from shaking and showing her fear and disgust.

"The sooner the better, honey. The sooner the better!"

Davis stepped away from the man and moved to

Ruth's side. "Are you crazy?"

Ruth didn't say anything; she merely turned and started out of the apartment.

"I'll call you in a week," she told Anson as they stepped out of the room and into the hallway.

"I'll depend on that, honey!" she heard as John slammed the door behind them.

They were silent all the way back to John's car. As they were driving along the Hollywood freeway, John asked: "Where you going to get the money?"

"I have a thousand saved—the rest I might be able to get from Carl. I'll *have* to!" Ruth told him.

"I should have killed him! I should have torn his apartment apart!"

That was the last thing he said until they had driven up to Carlton Turner's large Beverly Hills house. When the engine was dead, he turned and looked at Ruth. The expression in his eyes was strangely veiled.

"Ruth—I love you. Just remember that. I'm sorry about what I was responsible for getting you into. And I'll do—"

Ruth slid her arms around his neck and hugged close. "Don't, John. It wasn't your fault Anyway, you gave me my big break. And—maybe you've done something else for me. Proved that a guy can really like a tramp!"

"No, Ruth—*love* one."

He kissed her lips and then her forehead.

"Get the hell out of this car!" he ordered in a choked, husky voice.

Without a word Ruth slipped out of his arms and then out of the car. She watched as he drove down the street and turned the corner.

166

Strangely she almost loved him, Ruth realized as she turned and walked toward Carlton Turner's home. *Not the way a woman loved a lover—but more like a sister loved a brother.*

But she doubted that John loved her the way he'd said. No man could really love her the way a husband might love a wife; that, Ruth was sure, would always be denied her.

You're a forever mistress, she thought opening the front door of Carlton's home and stepping inside. *A professional tramp!*

CHAPTER TWELVE

Carlton Turner was waiting for her in the living room. He stood when she stepped into the room.

"Where have you been?" he demanded. "I was worried."

Ruth looked at him and felt a deep, welling emotion.

Yes, she thought, *it wasn't hard to love Carlton Turner.*

Then she remembered her meeting with Anson, and the threat of his blackmail and the money she had to get, some way, some how.

"Something came up," she told him, moving close to Carlton. "I'm sorry, honey." She slid her arms around his neck and brushed his cheeks against hers. "Love me?"

Irritation showed on his face and he pushed her away.

"What brought that on?" he snapped angrily.

"What's wrong with you?"

"Oh, nothing. Just that I waited at the office for you—and you didn't turn up. I thought we'd go out on the town. Celebrate the finishing of the picture—and the finishing of your romance with Jimmy Belmont!"

"I'm sorry. Really, Carl. Something—" she

168

broke off, realizing how impossible it was to tell the man what had really happened. "Carl, I need some money. It's something personal. Serious."

She sat down on the sofa and Carlton stood over her; a strange expression clouded his face.

Suddenly she realized how much she loved the man; how important he was to her.

If only he really loved her, she thought.

"How much?" Carlton asked. "Anything you want, dear." He sat down next to her. His hand caressed her thigh.

Ruth suddenly stood. "I could use a drink."

"Help yourself."

As she was pouring a small glass full of Scotch, Ruth wondered how she was going to get four thousand dollars. How would she tell Carlton about making a side-deal with a man like Anson; without revealing the truth?

She gulped the scotch and turned to face the man.

Carlton stared at her and said: "Something's bothering you, isn't it, Ruth. What? For God's sake tell me! I don't care what it is—I love you—and that's all that matters. I love you more than any woman in the world. That's a crazy fact! And that's saying something; because I never thought it would happen this way—on *any* way, for that matter." He stood and moved to her. His arm circled her waist. "Ruth—you don't realize I'm telling you the truth. I'll do anything for you. Believe me. Don't think you're unlovable! You're—"

"Stop, Carl. Please. You don't know what you're talking about. Sure. Maybe you love my body—and you love making love to me—and you *love* having me around. But don't talk about real love. Not to me!" She was as startled as the man by her sudden outburst.

The problems of Anson's blackmail deal had become as nothing next to the inner hurt that Carlton's declaration of love had caused. Suddenly nothing was important; because the only thing that had ever been important to her was the need to be loved. She had never realized that until this very moment. She had never understood the motives that had driven her from man to man, hating them; and then drove her to attain stardom in the Hollywood. Now she suddenly realized the driving forces that had moved her through life; the demanding pressures which had driven her. And she understood the hate she'd had for men, whom she had been sure could never give her the love she'd so desired in life.

And she realized how easy it was to hate Carlton Turner for mouthing the very things she'd always wanted to hear from a man who really felt them. She was sure that Carlton Turner was merely fooling himself; that he was trying to fool her into believing his fantasy.

"Nobody loves a tramp, Carl. So don't rub it in!" she cried, turning away and pouring herself another drink of scotch.

"Crap!" the man shouted. "And double crap! I've never heard such a thing. A real man doesn't really care what a woman *has* been in the past, all he's interested in is what she is, *now,* in the present! If he loves her, he'll forgive anything. *Anything at all!"*

Ruth smiled, turned and said the one thing she would never have thought possible to say: "You know why I was late getting home? Oh, but of course you don't. Well, take a good listen, mister high and mighty, lover-boy, Carlton Turner! A man named Allen Anson sent me a blackmail note. That's why!"

Carlton stared at her; puzzled "What are you talking about?"

"Before I met you I made a stag movie. A movie where I had sexual intercourse with a strange man who I never saw before or since. Mr. Anson wants $4,000 and half of everything I'll even make, and he'll hand over the films and negatives. Now what do you think about your high and mighty love for a real honest to goodness tramp?"

She stood there stunned at what she'd said. She watched the man's face whiten and his jaw grew hard. She watched as his eyes narrowed with anger.

Without a word, Ruth rushed out of the house, and down the street. The night air brushed her face, threading the tears along her cheek and down her neck. Her mind was screaming over and over again. What a fool she had been.

Why, why had she told him that? Why? Why? she cried oven and over. It had been insane. It didn't have logic or reason behind it.

Ruth turned a dark corner and kept running. She heard a car coming down the street behind her and ducked into a driveway.

The car crept slowly by and she recognized Carlton's face. After it had passed by, she started down the street again. It was a long time before she came to Sunset Boulevard and then walked down to the Strip. She went into the first bar and sat down on a barstool. She ordered a Martini. When it had been half finished she looked around the small cocktail lounge.

There were several single men sitting scattered around the place. For the first time in months she thought about picking up a man. The idea sent a strange thrill through her. There was a certain security to the idea; doing something she knew best; something at which she was a real professional.

A man's eye caught hers and held. She smiled, her expression invited.

Without waiting a moment longer she stood and walked over to him. It wouldn't take much conversation to get him out of the bar, she thought as she sat down beside him.

* * * * * * *

Ruth didn't know the name of the man anymore. He had introduced himself at the bar; but she had forgotten it as soon as he had given it.

Now she was in a small motel room, lying under his hungry caresses. She was drunk. And she felt nothing. But it was better than the agony she'd felt when rushing out of Carlton Turner's home.

The man's lips hungrily worked on one of her breasts and she felt only slight pleasure. Part of her wanted to run, get out of the room, away from him. Another just wanted to die there, merged in the past routine of using men to survive. That was what this really meant to her; control. She could kick this guy away and out.

Suddenly she pushed the man way. Furiously she struggled. But he was too strong and for a blurred moment she felt a dizziness, and confusion.

172

Something slapped her face, hard. Then distance blurred reality. She felt the sensation of a male in her and her lips repeating softly, over and over again, Carlton Turner's name.

Time blurred.

She was alone in the room. She didn't know where the man had gone; and she didn't care. It was better to be alone; to think; to try to find some sanity in her world.

It was still dark outside; it was still night and the world was asleep, unaware of the woman in the motel room, tormented by her memories of a life that had been spent in the arms of men who paid for sex. All the men had paid a price; but none the one that she had wanted.

Her price had been money or a helping hand along the way to stardom. But now even her movie career would be finished. She doubted that Carlton would even release the film; now. And certainly have nothing more to do with her. She's burned that bridge in one sweepingly foolish confession.

No, Ruth thought, *he would release it. There would be no way out of that!*

Then another thought iced its way into her awareness. Why had she tried to test his love? Why had she even bothered? It shouldn't have made that much difference to her. It was the kind of situation she'd have dreamed about a year before. But something inside had welled up to choke out reason.

Ruth suddenly wondered if it would be too late to pick up the pieces.

Carlton had come out searching for her; that much she was certain of. Maybe he didn't care about the picture she'd made for Anson; maybe he really did love her the way he said.

Then another thought occurred to Ruth. If he really had loved her, why hadn't he offered marriage?

Ruth laughed at that. She could accept the idea that a man might love her—for a while—but to marry her was something completely different.

A cold determination settled over Ruth. Realistically, all she had to do was accept things as they were and stop tormenting herself with romantic thoughts of love.

Hard line she was an ex-prostitute.

That thought nagged her. Ex—not a prostitute any more, not even a call-girl. A woman with an acting career ahead of her. With or without Carlton Turner. Once the film was released, and if it was as good as it appeared to be, then she would get offers—and there would be plenty of men to play out skillfully for her own purposes.

To hell with this love crap! She told herself. *Just be realistic! Make the most of what you have. You're better off than you were when you arrived in Hollywood, so stop crying like a spoiled little brat!*

She would return to Carlton's home and find out how things stood with him. If all that was left was a hard line business arrangement, so be it. She would try to pick up the pieces, and make the most of them.

* * * * * * *

The house looked dark, but when she let herself in, Ruth discovered that there was a small light on in the living room and Carlton Turner was sitting there, asleep. He was still dressed and his clothes were wrinkled.

Tip-toeing across the room, Ruth attempted to pass the man without waking him. She could talk to him the next morning.

But Carlton opened his eyes as she was opposite him.

For a moment he stared at her as if he couldn't believe what he was seeing.

Then suddenly he leaped to his feet.

For a moment Ruth thought he was going to do something violent. Then when his arms went around her, crushing her body to his, she felt a confusion of emotions shoot through her.

"Oh, God! I was scared I'd lost you forever. I went out of my mind!" Carlton's lips were frantically kissing her face, neck and then finally her mouth. "God! Never do anything like that again!"

After a little while, Carlton stepped back and looked at her; his face grew serious.

"You should have come to me right away about this Anson thing. I should be mad about that—but never mind it!" He took hold of her hand and led her across the room. "We're going on a little trip. I don't think you've ever been in Las Vegas, have you?"

Ruth froze. A hard lump tightened her throat so that it was impossible to talk for a long time.

Finally she said: "What are you talking about?"

"Well, first," he began, smiling tenderly down at her, "you can stop worrying about Anson. I paid him a visit with that Davis guy. We pulled out his teeth. Once he learned that I knew about the film, he put the make on me—I told him to shove his films—and warned him that if he didn't sell them to me, right away, I'd make sure there was a lot of trouble. Anson is just a small-time jerk—and he's scared. A neat two thousand gave me the film."

Alarm shuddered through Ruth. "What'd you do with them?"

"Burned them." He patted her cheek and lowered his lips to hers. "Ruth, you're a strange, mixed-up little kid, and it's about time you learned something about the facts of life and love and men!"

He pulled her closer and their lips met again. After a moment he said: "Oh, let's get the hell out of here!"

"Where—why—Las Vegas?" she stammered, not knowing what to say. Her head was spinning; she felt weak and excited, and didn't know really why.

"To get married, child! To get married! I told you that a man could love you—that I love you. What more proof do you need?"

He pulled her after him. It wasn't until they were already on the Sunset Strip that Ruth came out of her daze.

It didn't seem possible. Everything was happening too fast for her to adjust to.

"I don't get it?" she managed to say, looking lovingly at Carlton.

"Don't try."

"But I didn't know you *really*—"

"Meant it? That I loved you? I didn't know it until you walked out. I loved you—but I didn't realize how complete that love was until I thought I'd lost you."

"It's just happening too fast!" she cried, half

176

laughing and half crying. She wiped her eyes, but the tears kept coming through the laughter.

"Things will be happening fast from now on, dear," Carlton said, patting her hand. "Things are just beginning to happen to you—and they'll continue to happen. You've found a new life—and a new world—and someday maybe you'll forget the hell of what your past was."

Ruth finally gained control of her emotions and sat there beside the only man she had ever loved; the man who would soon be her husband. And the more she thought about her future, the dimmer the past seemed.

Yes, she thought happily, *maybe she would forget her past.*

Already it was hard for her to actually think of the things Ruth Browne had done as being the actions she had gone through. Last night had proven to her just how horrid that kind of experience was. It wasn't the kind of life she ever wanted to know again—she simply wanted to forget the past and live for the now and the future.

She leaned closer to Carlton as they drove onto the freeway. His arm folded around her. Neither of them moved for a long, long time.

When the sun started to rise on the eastern horizon, it looked down upon the new Ruth—the future Mrs. Carlton Turner. And she was completely happy for the first time in her life.

ABOUT THE AUTHOR

Charles Nuetzel was born in San Francisco in 1934, and writes:

"As long as I can remember I wanted to be a writer. It was a dream I never thought would materialize. But with the help of Forrest J Ackerman, who became my agent, I managed to finally make it into print.

"I was lucky enough not only in selling my work to publishers but also ending up packaging books for some of them, and finally becoming a 'publisher' much like those who had bought my first novels. From there it as a simple leap to editing not only a science-fiction anthology, but also a line of SF books for Powell Sci-Fi back in the 1960s. Throughout these active professional years I had the chance to design some covers and do graphic cover layouts for pocket books & magazines."

Much of his work in covers and graphics are a result of having had a father who was a professional commercial artist, and who did a number of covers for sci-fi magazines in the 1950s and later for pocket books—even for some of Mr. Nuetzel's books.

In retirement he has become involved in swing dancing, a long time lover of Big Band jazz. But more interestingly world travels have taken him (and his wife Brigitte) across the world, to Hawaii, Caribbean, Mexico, Kenya, Egypt, Peru, having a lifelong interest in ancient civilizations. His website is full of thousands of pictures taken during these trips.